HOME TO YOU

LACEY BLACK

KAYLEE RYAN

CHAPTER 1

Sebastian

Dinggg.

The final bell sounds, alerting the students of the end of the school day. "Don't forget to study chapter two on fractions. We'll have a test at the end of the week," I tell my final class as they start to shuffle for freedom.

"Umm, Mr. Hall?"

I turn to see Kallie Tucker, one of my algebra students, lingering in front of my desk.

"How can I help you, Kallie?"

She pops her gum and twists her long blonde hair the way girls seem to do when they flirt. "Sooo, I was just wondering," she says, leaning a little too far over my desk for my comfort level. "Do you tutor after school? I'm still having trouble with multiplying those fractions, and well, I thought if you're able to help me after cheerleading practice, it might help me, you know, get a better grade."

I swallow and inwardly groan.

Not the first time a student has asked for a little extra help in math. I'm not completely oblivious to what they all say about me. They call me *The Fox*. I'm a thirty-two-year-old high school teacher, the youngest male professional in the school. I'm surrounded by raging hormones all day long, but I've perfected the ability to ignore them all.

"Yeah, sorry, Kallie, I'm not available for tutoring. If you meet with Mrs. Holstein in the front office, she can help partner you up with after school help," I tell her as I slide the papers I have to grade tonight into my bag.

"Awww," she singsongs, her bottom lip jutting out in a pout. "Really?"

I give her a small smile. "Yeah, I'm sure. I have football after school every day," I remind her. It's not like she doesn't remember I'm the head football coach for Hope High School, home of the Tigers and pride of Southern Idaho. We have four straight playoff visits but are still looking for our first state title in school history.

"But what about after that?" she asks.

Sliding my laptop into the bag, I reply, "I'm unavailable after practice, Kallie. I take care of my daughter."

She coos and makes the kind of face you'd make to a baby. "Oh, that's right. Well, maybe another time," she replies before throwing a wink and a wave over her shoulder and leaving my room.

With a deep sigh, I flop back in my chair and relax. The door is still open, the chaos in the hallways spilling through my doorway. I've taught at Hope High since graduating from college a decade ago, back when I was young and thirsty to help change the world. I still very much want to do my part, but it's more taxing than ever before. The state is changing its guidelines for classroom work, putting more and more paperwork on the teachers.

If only the pencil-pushers at the Capitol understood what it really took to teach.

And for a shitty salary, at that.

"Ready, Coach?" Dallas, one of my cornerbacks, hollers from the doorway.

"I'm ready, Dallas. See you on the field," I reply as I get up, verifying I have everything before locking my classroom for the night.

Only a few students linger in the halls as I make my way down the longest corridor to the locker rooms. I have a small office in the back that smells like gym socks and mildew on a good day and as bad as rotten cheese on a bad one. Today, it's the latter.

I drop my stuff on the desk, grab my whistle and play-book, and head through the locker room. The players are there, hooting and hollering as they get ready for practice. Mondays are always film day. We'll start with a good warm-up and run some sprint conditioning, followed by a return to the locker room to watch Friday night's game.

We've only had two games, but we're sitting at a two and zero record. The first real challenge of the season is going to be this Friday. We'll play a damn tough Raiders team from neighboring Gleason, and while we went to the second round of playoffs last year, the Gleason Raiders went four games deep.

"Hey, Coach," James, my defensive line coach, says as I step outside and head out back to the practice field.

"Hey, James. How was your day?"

"Not too bad," he remarks, placing a line of cones at the fifty-yard line. James is a banker who played college ball two decades ago. He could have gone pro, too, if not for a knee injury his senior year of college.

The rest of my coaching team arrives as the players start

to file out of the locker room. In a small town like Hope, you have to look outside the school for coaching help. My team consists of two teachers, a county deputy, the highway road commissioner, a retired judge, and a banker, all with their own deep insight and love for the game of football. When I took over as head coach five years ago, I inherited the rest of the team, but I wouldn't trade any of them for the world.

I blow my whistle and the players line up. We've got both teams here today, varsity and the junior varsity. Mondays and Wednesdays, they practice together. Tuesdays and Thursdays, they split up and run drills and practice their own offense and defense. Saturday is weight training and team projects, and Sunday is their off day, though you'd find several of my boys in a weight room anyway. I've got a good group of kids here, and I'm anxious to see where they take us.

My senior captains work on stretches and warm-ups while the coaches and I discuss Friday night's game. "Carson had some great passes but was still a little slow out of the gun. I'd like to work on some more speed drills with him, getting him to bring the ball straight up to firing position, not windmilling it around like this," Coach Lehman says, demonstrating how much time is added to the play when Carson swings his arm around to get into position.

"I agree. I've been watching it, but it seems to be more consistent now than before. Let's work with him tomorrow with the O-line," I reply, watching as the last row of kids crosses the fifty-yard line.

"What do you want to do about Adam? I hear he's on the verge of failing English," Coach Haun, the only other teacher in the group, asks.

I shake my head. "We're like two full weeks into school. How is he almost failing already?" I ask, my eyes seeking out the young man in question. He's a big boy, one of my best linebackers, but he doesn't have much of a home life. His parents rarely come to support his games, and when they do, I'm pretty sure they're drunk. Adam struggles to get through school and works at a local gas station as an attendant as much as possible.

Coach Haun shakes his head. "Hasn't turned in two of the four assignments."

I blow out a big puff of air. "That'll do it. I'll talk to him after practice," I say, heading over to where the boys are grabbing a quick drink of water. I blow my whistle to catch their attention. As soon as they finish their drinks, the team throws on their helmets and meets me at the end zone.

We spend twenty minutes running sprints and a few drills, and the moment I tell them to get a drink, they all rip off their helmets and head for the water before filing back inside the locker room. The TV is there, ready to go for the remainder of practice. Each coach goes through key plays during last Friday's game while the players look on in concentration.

As soon as we're done, I slip back into my office, motioning for Adam to see me before he leaves. He arrives a few minutes later, sweaty from the late summer heat, and dressed in his work uniform. "Hey, Coach. You wanted to see me?"

"I did, Adam. Have a seat," I instruct, coming around to the front of my desk and sitting on the edge. "I hear you're missing a few assignments in English."

Adam drops his head and averts his eyes. "Yeah."

"You're on the bubble for eligibility, Adam, and I'm sure that's not what you want."

"Hell no, Coach!" he replies, his eyes alive with the fire I see on the field on Friday nights.

"I figured as much, but if you don't get your grade up a little, you risk the chance of not playing this week."

He sags against the old wooden chair. "Sorry, Coach. I'm trying, but my mom, she was gone a lot this last week, and Dad wasn't happy. I worked a lot to help cover some of the rent," he says, his eyes looking so much older than a young seventeen year old's should.

I crouch down in front of him so we're eye level. "You're a good boy, Adam. What you're doing to help your family is commendable, but you also have an obligation to your studies. You know my rules. In order to play, you have to be passing."

He swallows hard. "I know. I'll do better."

Something flashes in those soulful eyes. "If you need help with your homework, all you have to do is ask."

Adam gives me a small smile. "Thanks, Coach, but I'm sure I can figure it out."

I nod in reply and stand up, dismissing my player. Just as he reaches the door, I say, "Hey, if you ever need a place to chill for a bit, let me know. Actually, just stop by. You know where I live," I state. Adam is one of the handful of players who helped me move two years ago when I went through my divorce. "My door is always open."

Adam gives me a look full of relief, as if someone just threw him the lifeline he was desperately needing. "Thanks, Coach."

"Be good," I reply with a grin before he heads out of my office.

I sag against the desk again and run my hand through my hair. There's a printout from our administrator waiting, and I give it a quick once-over. It's still early in the season, early in the new school year, but eligibility problems are already plaguing the team. Not many, but it looks like three are currently teetering on the bubble, and another one is failing chemistry. I drop the paper in my bag, something for me to deal with tomorrow, and grab my stuff. A quick glance at the clock confirms it's time for me to head out.

I make sure the locker room is empty before turning off the lights and locking the door. The air is thick as I push the door and head for the back parking lot.

"Hello, Sebastian," one of the other math teachers, Mrs. Markley, says before slipping into her car.

"Hey, Claire." I wave as I make it to my car, setting my bag in the passenger seat.

The drive to my ex-wife's house is quick. The moment my car is parked, a little brunette with pigtails and a pink tutu flies down the steps and into my waiting arms. "Daddy!" Chloe hollers before pressing a sticky kiss to my cheek.

"What have you been eating? Jelly?" I ask, carrying her in my arms and heading inside.

"Jelly wiff peanut butter!" Chloe bellows, a wide toothy grin on her little face.

"And it's all over my counter," my ex-wife, Trina, says as we step through the door. "Come here and get your face washed," she adds as she starts to scrub the remnants of a PB&J off the counter.

I set my almost five-year-old down so she can go get cleaned up, and when I run my hand over my short beard, it comes back with something tacky. "I think you got jelly in my beard," I tell my daughter, who instantly starts to hysterically laugh. "It's not that funny," I grumble before throwing her a wink.

"Daddy likes jelly too!" Chloe shouts through her little fits of giggling.

When I turn to look at Trina, she throws me her washcloth, hitting me square in the face. This, of course, causes my little one to laugh even harder, resulting in laughter from her mother and me. "Thanks," I mumble as I clean off my face.

"You're welcome," she replies innocently.

Trina's dressed in scrubs, her hair pulled back in a tight ponytail, and her bag set on the counter by the door. She works as a nurse three nights a week at the local hospital, caring for those who come into the emergency room. It's actually where I met her not quite seven years ago. I had slipped on the bleachers at school, twisting my ankle pretty bad. I was afraid it was a break and ended up in the emergency room. Two X-rays and a phone number later, I left with crutches and a smile on my face.

We were able to make it work for a while, but by the time we realized we weren't right for each other, we had just celebrated our third wedding anniversary and had a three-year-old. I have to say, though, we had probably one of the most amicable divorces known to man. We both realized we wanted different things, neither wanting to hold the other back. Trina is recently engaged to a doctor at the hospital, and I've, well, I've spent a lot of alone time with my hand.

Sure, I've dated, if you can call it that, but I've had no luck since my divorce at finding someone who doesn't mind coming in second to a child or who understands the importance of my job. My schedule from August through October is crazy busy as I spend most days at school and nights at the football field. And when I'm not there, I'm with Chloe so Trina can work. I'm not an easy man to date. The women of Hope, Idaho, have proven that, but I still hold out hope I'll find the right woman sooner or later.

"Daddy, time to go!" Chloe says and heads over to get

her own bag. It's a pink one with a ballerina and her name embroidered on the front.

"Let's go, Princess Chloe," I say, clapping my hands together and reaching for her bag.

"Hey!" Trina bellows, grabbing our daughter's attention. Chloe takes off running and throws herself into her mom's embrace. "Love you, baby girl. I'll see you after preschool."

Chloe's with me tonight. I'll take her to preschool, which fortunately is across the street from the high school, and then Trina will pick her up afterward. It's not easy, but we make this co-parenting thing work.

"Have fun at ballet!" Trina hollers as we head out the door and to my truck.

Chloe buckles herself into her booster seat, talking a mile a minute about whatever happened at school today. Apparently, there was glue, a marble, and someone's nose, but I struggle to follow. I pull into the parking lot for Dancing in the Light, the small-town studio where Chloe takes beginners ballet every Monday. It's a thirty-minute class with Mrs. Simone, a local legend in the dance world. She's a former Broadway dancer herself before returning to her hometown, and many of her students have gone on to further their dance careers.

I swallow over the lump in my throat and ignore the familiar pang of regret that slides through my blood every time I'm here.

I take Chloe's hand and her bag and lead her to the front door. We step inside and find an available cubby for her belongings. She pulls out her slippers and carefully places them on her feet. I help her tie them, something else I've learned to do in the last few months, and make sure she's all set for class. Of course she is. She lives and breathes ballet. In her little pink tutu and white tights, I'd say she's ready to go.

"Did you hear about Mrs. Simone?" one of the dance moms asks as I sit down on the bench. Chloe goes over and starts to do some stretches before their class heads back.

"No, what happened?"

"She fell last week and messed up her hip. I think she has to have surgery," she says, sliding a little closer to me on the bench.

This is something else I've gotten used to.

Horny dance moms.

"Wow, that's terrible," I reply, subtly moving away from the mom a few more inches. "So who's teaching the class?" I ask, glancing over to check on Chloe.

"One of her former students," the mom replies, flipping through her phone. She sets her hand down on her leg, her fingertips very close to my own leg. The absence of a wedding ring is prominent, and I can't help but think she planned it. You know, flash your ringless finger in a single guy's face in hopes of getting an invite to coffee or maybe a date? I've seen it a hundred times, and no, I'm not just being cocky.

The Fox, remember?

"Well, I'm sure her former student will do just fine for a while. I'm grateful someone is able to help Mrs. Simone out," I reply as the class before ours starts to file out of the back studio.

The waiting room is bursting with activity as the previous class gathers their belongings to leave, and the new ones are awaiting their time to go back. I grab my phone and scan through a few emails while we wait. I wish I had my bag with me, but with the other moms hanging around and talking, I've learned it's hard to get any work done in here.

So, I stick to doing what I can on my phone and leave the paper grading to later at night when I'm home.

"That must be her," the mom says, elbowing me in the arm and grabbing my attention.

I look up to see a short, slender woman, her back to me. Her brown hair is long and curly but pinned high on her head. She's wearing black tights and a pink leotard that accentuates her perfect heart-shaped ass.

Why am I thinking about her ass?

Because it's a nice fucking ass and I haven't had any in about five months?

I clear my throat and watch, an odd sense of familiarity washing over me. The woman hugs one of the young students before the girl takes off out the door with her mother. Just as she turns around, Chloe runs up to me and gives me a hug. "I'll be back, Daddy."

"Okay, sweetheart. Have fun in class. Make sure you listen to your teacher."

"She's new. I don't know her name," my little one says, her expressive eyes so full of excitement and worry.

"It's okay. I'm sure she'll introduce herself."

"Are my little ballerinas ready?"

That voice.

I'd know it anywhere.

A chorus of "yeses" echoes through the waiting room as my blood swooshes through my ears. It can't be... can it?

I look up, shocked to see the face before me. Her green eyes are just as bright as I remember, her smile as wide and alluring. She's casually giving her new ballerinas high-fives while I worry about whether I'm actually breathing or not. My daughter's new ballet teacher grins warmly at her class and says, "I'm so excited to be here with you tonight. My name is Miss—"

"Haven." I finish her sentence.

Her gorgeous face registers shock first as our eyes meet for the first time since high school, since post-graduation when she left our hometown to pursue her dream of dancing, breaking my heart in the process. Haven Decker was my first girlfriend—my first everything—until it was time for her to go to Juilliard.

Leaving me behind.

"Sebastian," she says, gaping at me from across the small room.

I close my eyes for the briefest second, yet my mind fills with images of a time gone past. Haven wrapped in my arms, naked and beneath me. Her telling me she loved me more than anything, wanting to start our adult life together as soon as we graduated.

But then that letter came. The acceptance she didn't think she'd receive.

The one that took her three-quarters of the country away from me, never to return to our small Idahoan town.

Until today.

Haven Decker is back, and more gorgeous than ever before.

I'm in so much trouble.

CHAPTER 2

Haven

Keep breathing. Keep breathing. Keep breathing. I keep repeating the words over and over in my head. I knew this would happen. When I agreed to step in for Mrs. Simone Baker, I knew there was a chance I would run into Sebastian. Hope is a small town, and I understood it was inevitable. I just didn't realize it would be today, here at the dance studio with a bunch of horny dance moms drooling over him.

Speaking of drool, my hand rests against my chin as I check myself as discreetly as I possibly can. I'm good, but I'm still frozen in place. A dozen sets of little eyes watch me intently, and all I can do is stare at him.

What is he doing here?

"Chloe."

Shit! Did I say that out loud?

He points to one of the littles in a pink tutu and white tights. The little girl gives me a wave and a shy smile, and those hazel eyes, the eyes so much like her daddy's seem to shine like beacons. "She's my daughter."

He has a daughter. Of course he does. I knew this about him. Hope, Idaho, is a small town, and when I say small, I mean your-next-door-neighbor-knows-when-you-go-to-the-bathroom small. Everyone knows everybody, and bless their hearts, they like to stick their noses into your business. Case in point, the horny dance moms are hanging on our every word. Many of them have wedding rings that adorn their left hands, but that doesn't stop them from giving me the evil eye or looking at Sebastian like they could eat him alive.

Not that I blame them.

Sebastian Hall is the epitome of tall, dark-haired, and handsome. His hazel eyes are mesmerizing, and the beard he's sporting, well, let's just say it's not just the horny dance moms who have noticed. When I left, he was a boy, and now, Sebastian is all man.

"Haven?"

"Sorry." I shake out of my thoughts. "Hi." I wave awkwardly and turn my attention to the tiny dancers. "All right, ladies, are we ready to dance?" I ask them.

Cheers break out, and they run to the bar to start their stretches. At five, they're just learning the basics. I thought tonight would be a breeze, my first classes as I fill in for Mrs. Baker. That's what I get for thinking.

I don't turn to look at Sebastian, and I don't let my eyes wander to the moms I'm sure are still vying for his attention. I keep my laser focus on the class, on the little girls who are here to learn to be a ballerina—every little girl's dream. It was my dream, and it came true. I've made sacrifices for my career, and looking back, there are some things I wish I would have fought harder for.

Some people.

One person.

Sebastian.

I wish I would have fought for us. We could have made it work. We were young and in love, and despite the odds of the distance stacked between us, I should have fought harder. My biggest regret in life is walking away from him. We had our future mapped out, and then I got the letter that changed the course we were on.

For thirty minutes, I feel eyes burning the back of my head, but I refuse to turn around. I'm not ready to face him, to face our past. "Ladies, you did an amazing job. Thank you for being such great students," I praise them.

"Thank you, Miss Haven," they singsong. My heart swells, and I give them a grin, letting them know that their thank-yous make me happy.

"Will you be our teacher next week too?" one of them, a little blonde girl, asks.

"Yes. I'll be here until Mrs. Simone is feeling better."

"We miss her, but you are really nice," a little redhead informs me. She looks over at her mom and waves before turning back to me. "And you're really pretty."

"Thank you. Now, make sure you have all your things, and practice your balance by standing on one leg this week."

The next few minutes are a flurry of activity as they swarm me for goodbye hugs and race off to their parents. I have to face them, have to face him. There is no getting out of it.

Taking a deep breath, I turn and slowly walk toward the entryway. "Thank you, the girls all had a great night," I say in general, hoping that will be sufficient enough.

"Hi, I'm Sara. This little one is mine. Please give Mrs. Simone our well wishes."

"I most definitely will." I hold my hand out for her. "It's

nice to meet you, and my name is Haven. I actually grew up taking classes here." I give her a kind smile.

"You're a legend around here." Sara smiles. "I better get this one home. See you next week." She waves over her shoulder. Her daughter, whose name I did not catch, does the same as she skips to try and keep up with her mother's stride.

A few more of the moms introduce themselves. There is only one who appears to be sizing me up. I plaster a fake smile on my face and say all the right things. That's what I'm supposed to do—remain professional at all costs. On the inside, I'm irritated that she thinks she's good enough for Sebastian. He's one in a million and deserves better than a married woman. He deserves everything.

"Daddy, let's go." Chloe has her tiny hand in his as she stares up at him with absolute adoration.

"In a minute, sweetie. Daddy just needs to talk to Miss Haven for a minute."

"I was really good," she assures him.

"Of course you were, Chloe," I jump in. It's just the three of us left in the dance studio. "Your daddy and I used to go to school together." That's the best way I can describe it to a five-year-old. I'm sure neither Sebastian nor his ex-wife would be none too happy with me telling her that her daddy was my first everything and that I broke both of our hearts all those years ago.

"It was more than that." Sebastian's deep voice echoes throughout the quiet room.

I nod because there's not much more I can say. It was more, so much more, and I ruined it. Ruined us.

"Have you had dinner?" I stare at him in shock. Is he asking me to dinner?

"Oh, Daddy, can we get pizza, please, please?" Chloe asks, dancing on the balls of her feet.

"I don't know, sweet pea. Do you think that you can convince Miss Haven to have dinner with us?"

I suck in a breath at his words. Sure, I should have seen it coming a mile away with his question, but the actual invite and my heart wishing it to be true are two different things. "I don't want to impose."

"Well, Chloe, looks like it's leftover meatloaf for us."

"Yuck, Miss Haven, please, oh please, will you eat with us so we can have pizza? I don't want meatloaf." She sticks out her little tongue and shakes her head.

"You love my meatloaf." Sebastian stares down at his little girl who looks just like him.

"Not like I love pizza, Daddy." She puts her little hands on her hips, and I can't help but smile.

"What do you say, Haven? Have dinner with us?"

I never could refuse those hazel eyes. "Let me get my coat." I don't bother to try and tell him that I have a boyfriend. I was never good at pretending anyway. In this town, I know he already knows about my broken relationship. That's the issue with following your dreams to be a big star on Broadway. Your life is no longer your own. The tabloids snatch up any tiny shard of gossip they can get their hands on to sell papers. Unfortunately, that was me about six months ago.

I'd finally made it. I was cast in the leading role, but during rehearsals, I turned wrong, and my ankle gave out on me. It was a bad sprain. Bad enough that the doctors put me off work for eight weeks. You've heard the saying the show must go on? Well, that's exactly what happened. My understudy stepped up to fill my role, not just professionally but personally as well. Tiffany did so guilt-free, as did Leonard.

He didn't even bother to break it off with me. Instead, he let me catch them in my old dressing room.

Shaking out of my thoughts, I slip my arms into my coat, grab my purse and keys, and shut off the lights in the office area. "I'll, um, just follow you there." I hold up my keys. I'm acting like this is my first time in front of a man before. Then again, it kind of is. At least this man. Adulthood has been very good to him.

"I can bring you back to your car," Sebastian says, helping Chloe into her coat.

"No, really. It's fine. I can follow you. That will save you a trip."

"Haven."

"Really, Bash it's fine." The old, familiar nickname slips past my lips. It's been over ten years since I've seen him, but standing here with him and his daughter, it feels like I'm living in two different worlds: the past and the present.

His eyes soften. "Fine." With Chloe's hand clutched in his, they turn for the door. The two of them stand on the sidewalk while I lock up. "Hope Town, you remember where it is?" he asks.

He's not trying to be a dick, but the question stings all the same. "I know the way," I assure him.

With a nod, he motions for me to walk with them. He and Chloe are parked next to me. He waits until I'm buckled in before lifting Chloe into the back seat of his truck. I watch them through my tinted windows as he talks to her, looking in his rearview mirror. Once he's satisfied, I'm assuming that she's all buckled in, he gives his horn a quick beep. I take that as my cue to go. He always was protective, making sure I got home safe, opening doors for me, things like that. I wonder if he's still that same man? Has time changed him? From my limited interaction, my guess is no. If anything, it's made him even more protective, especially now that he's a father.

The drive is a short one, and luckily there are only two other cars in the parking lot when we pull in. I'm not embarrassed to be seen with Sebastian or his daughter, but the rumor mill is not something I'm looking forward to. I'm sure that's the last thing he wants his daughter to hear either.

"Daddy, can I play the games?" Chloe asks as he lifts her from the truck.

"After you eat all of your dinner." He settles her on his hip and places his hand on the small of my back, leading us into the restaurant.

I have to blink back the tears that threaten to spill. This could have been our life. Chloe could have been our little girl. We planned to have at least three, and all before we were thirty. We wanted to be able to be young and keep up with them. My thirty-second birthday was over three months ago. Just another reminder of something we lost by my leaving town.

Once we're inside, Sebastian leads us to a quiet booth in the back corner. It sits directly next to the games, so it more than likely won't be quiet for long. "This way I can watch her," he explains. Did I forget to mention, this is also the booth we used to snag any chance we could when we were dating? The games were in the front of the restaurant at that time, and this was truly the quietest secluded table here. We would snuggle on one side of the booth and talk about where our life was going. We were so young and so in love.

"Hi, welcome to Hope Town Pizza," a teenage girl greets us once we're settled. "Tonight's special is a large three-topping with breadsticks."

"You good with just cheese and pepperoni?" he asks me.

"That's perfect." I don't mention that I've not eaten a

slice of pizza since the day I left town. I've heard NY style pizza is great, but as a dancer, I'm constantly watching my weight. Even after Tiffany took my place, and I was resting my ankle, I counted every calorie. I never stopped the habit. Not to mention, I need to decide what to do with my career. I'm dancing again, but just to stay in shape. I've not been back to the company, not with Leonard and Tiffany flaunting their budding relationship. I thought that I missed dancing, being in the spotlight on stage. I convinced myself I would come home, see my family, and then go back. However, I've been back in Hope for three days and spending time with my parents, and now this, visiting my old stomping grounds, I'm not so sure I missed dancing as much as I thought I did.

"You're miles away," Sebastian says, placing his hand over mine. I glance to his side, and he nods toward the games. "I caved," he says with a shrug. "Penny for your thoughts." He keeps his hand over mine.

"I thought I missed it," I blurt. "After my injury, I thought I wanted to go back."

"And now?"

"I miss home." *I miss you.*

"I thought New York was home?" Those hazel eyes of his bore into mine.

"I lived there, but this place, this town, it will always be home to me." *You will always be home to me.* I want to say the words, but that's not fair to him. He has a life here. He's settled. He doesn't need me coming in and making things messy.

"There is something special about this town," he muses.

"Tell me about you," I say, removing my hand from under his when the waitress drops off our drinks. She sets a glass of water in front of me, as well as a glass of root beer.

"I wasn't sure how much you were willing to cheat, so I ordered you both."

"Thank you." I grab a straw, peel it out of the wrapper, and slip it into the glass of root beer. I take a long pull and fight the urge to sigh. I've missed pop. "Start talking, Hall." I point at him and wrap my lips back around my straw for another drink.

"Well, you're looking at the head football coach of the Hope Tigers." He grins. "I also teach high school math."

"Hot teacher." I smile. "I'm sure your female students love you."

He rolls his eyes and groans. "Some of them are so over the top, and they don't care who knows it. I swear, I worry about their home lives." He glances over at Chloe, which has me doing the same. She's perfectly content sitting on her stool playing Pac-Man.

"Meh." I wave him off. "Most of them are just horny teenage girls with a hot teacher fantasy."

"You sound like you could be speaking from experience?" He raises his eyebrows.

"A girl never tells her secrets," I tease.

"I thought I had all of your secrets?" His tone is teasing, but there is an underlying level of hurt in his words.

"What else?" I ask.

"Let's see. Trina and I met nearly seven years ago. We dated, and she ended up pregnant. We got married and tried to make a go of it for Chloe. We divorced two years ago."

"I'm sorry."

"Don't be. All three of us are happier. Trina and I realized we were better off as friends and co-parents. We both want what's best for our daughter, and that's not us being married. She's actually engaged to a nice guy."

"Wow. That's amazing. The two of you should write a book on how to co-parent the right way. I commend you both."

He nods. "What about you?"

"Not much to tell. I'm sure you heard about my injury and my fall from grace?"

He grimaces. "I know that everything I read and everything that passes the rumor mill is not true."

"Normally, I would agree with you, but this time it was all spot on. Except for the fact that I caught them in my bed. It was actually my dressing room."

"Ouch," he says.

"Pretty much."

"Are you home to stay?"

"No. At least I don't think so. To be honest, the last six months I've felt... lost." Longer if I'm really being honest, but I keep that to myself.

"I'm glad you're here." He reaches for my hand, but our waitress arrives with our breadsticks. "Chloe, come and eat."

"Okay, Daddy."

"She's such a happy little girl. You and your ex should be proud. You're doing an amazing job with her."

"Do you have kids, Miss Haven?" Chloe, the very observant five-year-old, asks.

"No. No kids."

"How come?"

I glance at Sebastian, and he's watching me as if he wants to know the answer as well. I decide to be as honest as I can without telling her the gritty details. "To have kids, you have to be married and in love." Not one-hundred percent accurate but I get a subtle nod from Sebastian, so I know I've said the right thing.

"Who do you love?" she asks, taking a huge bite of a breadstick.

Your father. My breathing catches in my chest, and I realize that my offhand thought really isn't offhand at all. It's been ages since I let myself think about my time with Sebastian, but being home, sitting here with him, it's all coming back with a flourish, and I know that I will always love him. There will always be a huge place in my heart for Sebastian.

"I loved a man once," I tell her. "He was very special to me."

"Did you marry him?"

"No, sweetie. I moved away, and we never got our chance." I refuse to look at Sebastian as I grab a breadstick from the basket and shove a huge bite into my mouth.

"Aw, man," she replies. "You're so pretty, and you should marry my daddy." She turns to look at Sebastian. "Daddy, you need to love Miss Haven so you can get married."

I smile at her. "That's not exactly how it works, Chloe, but thank you for the compliment."

"She's pretty, right, Daddy?" Chloe asks him.

"She's beautiful. Always was," Sebastian says. There's heat in his hazel eyes, and they're focused on me.

"Would you like some sauce?" I ask Chloe.

"Oh, I forgot it." She giggles, and her previous request for her father to marry me is already forgotten. At least I hope it's forgotten.

For the rest of dinner, Chloe controls the conversation. She asks me lots of questions about dancing, and thankfully no more talk about marrying her dad. The three of us polish off the breadsticks and the large pizza, and I have two root beers, with zero regrets. It is the absolute best meal I've had in ages.

When I try to give him money, Sebastian gives me his "don't argue with me" look, and it makes me smile. Some things never change. We exit the restaurant the way we entered with Chloe on her daddy's hip and his hand at the small of my back. He leads me to my car and waits for me to get inside.

"Give me your phone." He holds his hand out. I don't bother to argue. I know what he's doing, and I'm okay with it. It's been far too long since my phone has held the contact name, Sebastian. "There." He hands it back to me. "Now I have yours too. I'll call you."

I nod. This is eerily familiar yet so very different. "Thank you for dinner. Miss Chloe, don't forget to practice your balance," I say, putting my dance instructor hat back on.

"Oh, I won't. See you next week, Miss Haven." With a wave, they step away from my car, and I settle behind the wheel, shutting the door behind me. Just as before, he gives me a short beep, letting me know to pull out, and I do. He follows me nearly to my parents' place. I have no idea if it's out of his way, but I do know that my heart is squeezing in my chest, and there's emotion clogging my throat as the memories of what we had and what we lost filter through my mind.

CHAPTER 3

Sebastian

"Daddy, I want to be a dancer like Miss Haven when I grow big," Chloe says as I tuck her into bed and reach for her favorite stuffed chick.

"Sweetheart, you can be anything you want. Being a dancer is going to take a lot of hard work and determination, but you can do it," I reassure her, sliding the yellow animal under the blanket.

"What's deternation?" she asks, those hazel eyes gazing up at me in question and wonder.

"Determination. It means you're set in your decision or focused to get something done. Like when you want cookies for dessert and you're determined to get them," I tell her with a smile.

Her own grin sweeps across her face. "I want cookies for dessert! I'm deternammed."

I chuckle at her insistence. "You had a fudge pop before your bath. That's plenty of dessert for tonight." I pull the blankets up and bend down to kiss her cheek. I can smell the strawberry shampoo she insists on using, and the fruitiness of her body wash.

Chloe yawns and snuggles the chick close. "Can I get a baby chickie, Daddy?"

I inwardly groan at her simple question. This is just another thing my darling daughter has been mighty determined at. She wants a baby chick, and every time she asks for one, I get closer and closer to giving in. No, I don't know jack shit about raising chickens, but if my baby girl wants a chicken, well, I'm willing to learn. Besides, there are resources I can use locally to find out what I need to know. Haven's parents actually live on a small farm on the edge of town. They have horses, a few goats, and some chickens and ducks. They sell the eggs and vegetables at the local farmers market.

"We'll see, sweetheart. You need to go to sleep," I tell her, standing up.

"I not sleepy," she whispers as her eyes fall closed.

Smiling, I walk quietly toward the door. "Night, baby girl. Sweet dreams."

"Night night, Daddy. Love you."

My heart soars with happiness at her words. "Love you too."

I don't pull the door closed completely, but enough to ensure it's quiet in her room. I head straight for the laundry room and toss the load of dirty towels into the washing machine. Once in the kitchen, I gaze out over the backyard through the window above the sink. Any remaining light from the sun is almost gone, and night is closing in. My mind, of course, returns immediately to Haven. I wonder if she loves starry night skies as much as she used to.

I think back to how she looked earlier this evening. Her

long, curly hair piled high on her head. Her shapely body accentuated by a sexy leotard. Those intoxicating green eyes that used to gaze up at me with so much love and trust when she was naked beneath me. Adult Haven is everything I imagined her to be, and I'm pretty sure my cock agrees, if the hardness in my pants is any indication.

Haven and I used to do everything together. Most of my teenage memories involve her in one form or another. We were young when we got together, just barely sixteen, and very quickly, my world became wrapped in hers. We used to cruise the country roads in my old beat-up truck, listening to old Waylon and Willie songs, her snuggled up beside me in the center of the bench seat. Dances and football games, pep rallies, and movie dates. At the time, I thought I'd have her forever.

Until that acceptance letter to Juilliard.

There was no way I could tell her no. No way I would ask her to stay. She had one dream, and that was to dance. This was the biggest opportunity of her life, and I refused to stand in the way of it, even though I wanted to. I wanted her to stay with me, but deep down, I knew she'd regret it and resent me in the process. So, at eighteen years of age, I did the hardest thing I've ever done.

I let her go.

I know what everyone else said. We could have tried a long-distance relationship, but I knew it wouldn't work. Not when our lives were practically on two sides of the continent. I was going to a state college to receive my teaching degree. There was no way in hell I could afford to do that in New York, not with my parents struggling to foot the bill here in Idaho. It was going to cost me almost double to move, and I refused to do that to them.

I stayed behind and went to school, partying a little and

enjoying my college experience. But more often than not, she was on my mind. I wondered how she was doing in school, how she adjusted to the grueling work schedule that went with one of the top dance schools in the world. I was so fucking proud of her, even though I wasn't with her.

Still am.

My hands tighten on the counter as I think back to all the bullshit she's endured lately. First, the accident on set, which put an immediate halt to her bright career while she rehabbed. Then the news of her live-in boyfriend cheating on her with a much younger version of herself while she was licking her wounds.

Leonard.

What kind of name is Leonard anyway?

And who the fuck cheats on an amazing woman like Haven Decker?

A scumbag, douche nozzle, that's who.

I push off the counter and head to the living room. I hit the remote power button just to fill the room with white noise before grabbing my bag. Dropping on the couch, I glance up to see the commentators discussing this week-end's college football games, predicting who will win in the Big Ten Conference.

I pop a red felt pen out of the bag and glance down at the first paper. I work through the problems, marking which ones are incorrect, but it takes me longer than usual. Grading papers is something I generally enjoy, but tonight, I just find it mundane and difficult. My attention keeps going right back to the one person I should probably stop thinking about.

Yet, here I am, once again, letting my mind be consumed by Haven Decker.

I toss the papers aside, chastising myself for only getting

three finished. I jump up, my legs needing to move, and head outside. The night air holds a touch of humidity and warmth as I lean against the railing and take a deep breath. I try to ignore my erection, but it's hard.

Pun intended.

All I can think about is her. The excitement and shock that raced through me as I looked up into her green eyes for the first time in more than a decade. Inviting her to dinner, and her accepting. How her scent was just as familiar as the smile on her face. She knew how to light up a room, just by entering it. She could completely disarm me with just the slightest touch of her soft, delicate fingers on my skin.

My cock aches with need as those sweet memories flood my mind.

She was my first love, my first everything.

And now she's home, even if for a short time. I have no clue what to do about that. All I know is spending just a few minutes in her presence feels like a homecoming. Like my soul has finally reconnected with its other half. And that's just after spending an hour with her.

I glance down and groan in frustration. Both sexual and otherwise. There's no way my cock will just magically subside until I take care of it. Haven is too fresh on the brain. I head inside, making sure the doors are all locked. A quick peek at Chloe confirms she's still out cold, so I proceed to my bedroom. Grabbing the first pair of boxers in the drawer, I then slip into my en suite bathroom and lock the door.

I crank up the water as hot as I can stand and toss my dirty clothes in the hamper. The room fills with steam, the mirror covered, which is probably a good thing. I'm not sure I want to see my reflection right now. It'd probably display a combination of resolve, guilt, and desire, all rolled into one.

The water stings my back, but I ignore it. Leaning my forearms against the cool tile, I let the heat cascade over my taut body. My groin throbs, an unpleasant reminder of the longing I still possess for the first woman I ever loved. Her image has me taking my swollen cock in my hand and giving it a squeeze. Lust bolts through my veins as I close my eyes and succumb to the sensation.

My hand moves, slowly at first, as I think about Haven. Her plump, pouty lips I'd love to see wrapped around my cock, the feel of her hand replacing my own, and the pleasure in her eyes as she gazes up at me. My movements start to quicken as I recall all those times she cried out, my name on her lips, as she came all over my cock.

That familiar tingle slides up my spine, and I know this'll be over quickly. My body is like a lit fuse, sizzling and crackling as it gets closer and closer to detonation. The release I've been craving is right there, and all it takes is the sweetness of her name on my own lips to send me over the edge.

I come so hard, it steals my breath, but I don't stop moving my hand until I'm completely drained of energy. My body sags against the tile, the too-hot water all but forgotten. My body feels sated, but I know it'll be short-lived. With Haven back in town, I'll be walking around in a perpetual state of arousal, no doubt.

I wash up, letting the heat relax my weary muscles. When I get out of the shower, I grab the last clean towel, a reminder I need to flip the wash over to the dryer before I go to bed. Otherwise, I'll have nothing but a hand towel to dry off tomorrow morning, and that'll suck ass. I slip on the boxers and brush my teeth, careful to avoid my own reflection in the mirror. I should feel guilty for picturing my daughter's ballet teacher while jacking off in the shower, but I just can't seem to find the urge.

The washer has completed its cycle, so I toss the towels and some dryer sheets into the dryer and turn it on. As I head back to the kitchen, I fill a glass with water and spy my phone on the counter. It's just lying there, taunting me for some weird reason. The clock is approaching ten, way past an appropriate time to reach out.

Yet, here I am, reaching for my phone and swiping the screen.

A photo of Chloe and me from earlier in the summer appears on the screen and makes me smile. I took it at the zoo in front of the monkey enclosure. Her chocolate ice cream smile is full of exhaustion and excitement from her first big outing to see zoo animals. By the time we had to go, I was carrying her out of there. I remember she passed out before we even got out of the parking lot.

I know I probably shouldn't do this, yet I still pull up a blank text screen and type in her name.

Me: Just checking to see if you got home okay.

Before I can set the device back down on the counter, the little bubbles appear, and I'm suddenly holding my breath for her reply.

Haven: Uhhh, yeah, like two and a half hours ago. *insert smirk emoji*

Me: Well, I got busy with Chloe and bath time and one story turned to two...

. . .

Haven: It's a good thing I wasn't kidnapped. He'd have a horrible head start.

I roll my eyes at her sass as I picture her sitting on her bed, typing that message.

Me: Anyway, thanks for having dinner with me and Chloe tonight.

Haven: It was my pleasure. And like I said earlier, you didn't need to pay.

Me: Just say thank you, Have.

Haven: Thank you, Have.

Me: Smartass...

When she doesn't reply right away, I figure end this while I'm ahead.

Me:I'll let you get to bed. Just checking on you.

· · ·

Haven: To make sure I got home okay. Got it.

Me: Night, Have

Haven: Goodnight, Bash

There's something incredibly familiar and easy with our communication, and I realize it would be so simple to fall into old routines. Not that it would be a bad thing...

I double-check the door locks, leaving the small light on above the sink. It's not too often Chloe gets up in the middle of the night, but when she does, it's for a drink of water. Only when I'm sure everything is set, do I finally head to bed, without completing my grading work. Oh, well. I'll just wrap it up during my third period prep hour.

As I climb into bed, I flip on the television. I don't need it to sleep, but the distraction would be nice. Yet the longer the program plays, the less I focus on what they're saying and more on a certain green-eyed brunette with an angelic smile. The one who makes my heart beat like a fucking drum in my chest.

The one who may still own a sliver of said heart.

* * *

"Can I stay out here with you?" Chloe asks from the side-lines as the team takes off for the locker room.

Sighing, I give her a pointed look. "You know you can't, sweetheart. I need to focus on the game when I'm out here."

"I can help you, Daddy!" she insists, puffing out her lower lip in a perfect pout.

"You're a great help, sweetie, but not during the game. I'll never focus if you're on the sidelines with me. You're gonna sit with Mommy in the bleachers." We both glance up to see my ex-wife and her fiancé sitting in their usual spot in the stands.

Chloe sighs. "Fine," she grumbles, reaching out her hand for me to take. "But I can still come out with you, right?"

"Of course you can," I reassure her, knowing this is one of her favorite parts of Friday nights.

We walk together to the locker room, stopping before we hit the doorway. "Look, Daddy! It's Miss Haven!"

I glance toward the entrance to see the very woman I can't stop thinking about walking alongside her father. She's carrying a thin blanket to sit on, and her face lights up when she sees my daughter. Chloe starts waving emphatically, causing Haven to do the same. My heart sort of skips around in my chest knowing she's here. I haven't seen Haven Decker at a football game since our senior year, the last game of the season. I received a kiss after my final high school game, and I can't help but think about what it would be like to have that again tonight.

After throwing Haven and her dad a wave, I knock on the locker room door to make sure they're ready. They know Chloe is coming in, so chances are the players are prepared for her arrival. One of my assistant coaches hollers, letting me know we can enter the locker room.

Inside, my team takes a knee and waits for me to speak. "Tonight, we're two and oh, but that doesn't matter. Focus on this game. Gleason is a tough team, but we're smarter, tougher in the long game. Watch for the blitz and the outside linebackers." I look around and make eye contact with as many as I can. "Captains, bring in your team."

They all jump up and gather in the center of the room. I take Chloe to the door and wait for the four senior captains to pump up the guys. When they're ready, they line up at the door, an electricity buzzing through the room I can feel coursing through my own veins. I love this feeling, this moment. The few moments right before we take the field, where the entire game is before us, the win for the taking.

When I get the cue, I step out of the door. The field is before us, the cheerleaders forming a tunnel of pompoms that lead to a paper sign. Each game we choose a different senior to lead us on the field, and I wait until Liam gets in place. Our school fight song starts, and I slap him on the shoulder pad, signaling it's time. "Let's go!" he yells before taking off out the door, the rest of the team hot on his heels.

The crowd erupts as the boys take the field, Chloe and me right behind them. The rest of the coaches are hot on our heels. We wait on the sidelines for the players to run through the paper banner and join me. They form a circle around Chloe, always making sure she's a part of this moment. "Tigers, are we weady?" she hollers, jumping up and down with the boys.

We all shove our right hands in the center, Chloe's little arm extended up in the middle. "Tigers on three. One, two, three..."

"Tigers!" the team echoes into the Friday night lights.

I take my daughter's hand and lead her toward the stands. Instantly, she spots her mom, who starts waving, but my eyes are drawn upward. Two rows up from where my ex-wife sits is my ex-girlfriend. They've never met, yet here they are so fucking close together. Chloe notices Haven too and waves up at her too.

"All right, sweetheart, head up to sit with Mommy, okay?"

"Bye, Daddy," she says, heading for the bleacher stairs. "Go Tigers!" she adds before she even hits the third step.

I watch as everyone gives her plenty of room, some even greeting her by name as she goes. It makes me feel good how the community has embraced her as much as they have me. When she reaches Trina, I go to turn, but my eyes slip a quick glance up to Haven. She smiles and flutters her fingers in a wave before turning her attention to Chloe, who has turned around and is begging for her to notice.

Grinning, I turn back in the direction of the game and slip on my headset. My captains come off the field after winning the coin toss. It's time to forget about my daughter and the sexy woman from my past in the bleachers and how easy it would be to fall into something I'm not sure either of us are ready for. It's time to focus on the game, on the next four quarters of football.

Easier said than done.

CHAPTER 4

Haven

My eyes are glued to Sebastian the entire game. I couldn't tell you what the score is or how well either team is doing. I can tell you that he's run his hands through his thick locks at least a half a dozen times and that about two minutes ago, something good happened if the way he was jumping up and down and smiling is any indication. I've spent the entire first half watching him, thinking about how this would be my life if things were different. If I'd made different choices.

"I'm going to grab a drink. You want anything?" my father asks from beside me.

"No, thank you."

"You enjoying the game?" he asks, smirking.

Busted. "Of course," I reply easily.

"Uh-huh." He chuckles as he stands to walk past me.

"Miss Haven, Miss Haven." I hear a sweet little voice

that I recognize instantly. "Mommy, it's her. It's Miss Haven. Can we go say hi?" Chloe asks her mom.

Her mom laughs and stands with Chloe's hand in hers as they walk up the two steps to my row. "Hi, I'm Trina, the little one's mom. I've heard a lot about you." She gives me a friendly smile and offers me her hand.

"Nice to meet you."

"She's daddy's friend," Chloe tells her mother.

I try not to cringe. I know Sebastian said they have a good relationship, but this still feels awkward as hell. "We went to school together."

"Oh, you're *that* Haven." Trina nods like she's finally found the missing piece to a puzzle she's been trying to finish.

"That's me." I smile. I hope it appears to be reassuring and not show the internal freak-out I'm having.

"Chloe has been practicing her balance," Trina comments with a kind smile.

"Momma, I tolded Miss Haven that she should love my daddy so they can get married like you and Dave."

My face heats from embarrassment, and I want to crawl under the bleachers. "Honey, it's not that simple," Trina tells her daughter with a soft, loving motherly voice. She glances at me and shrugs.

"Dat's what Daddy said too." She crosses her arms and juts out her bottom lip.

"Hey." Trina bends her knees so that she's eye to eye with her daughter. "You know that Daddy, Mommy, and Dave all love you very much. One day when Daddy falls in love, you'll have a stepmommy to love you just as much. These things take time, sweet girl. Love isn't something you rush." She stands back to her full height. "It was nice to meet you. I promised this one some popcorn."

"Bye, Miss Haven." To my surprise, Chloe engulfs my legs in a hug. "Can we have pizza again?" she asks, her eyes full of hope.

"You're going to have to ask your daddy about that," I tell her.

"Oh, he'll say yes. He was really smiley when you ate pizza with us." With that, she takes her mother's hand, and they continue on to get their popcorn.

* * *

The Tigers take home the win, and the electricity of the crowd is contagious. It feels like home. I have so many memories at this stadium, and tonight brought them all back with a vengeance. The only difference is instead of Sebastian making the plays, he's calling them.

"You ready, sweetheart?" Dad asks from his spot next to me on the bleachers. We sat for a while, letting some of the crowd thin out.

"Yes." Standing, I gather the blanket I brought for us to sit on, and we begin to descend the bleachers.

"Miss Haven!" I hear Chloe's voice call out for me. Turning, I see her standing with both of her parents. I offer her a wave and keep on walking.

My heart is in my throat. I know that they're divorced, but seeing them together with their daughter... That should have been me.

"Haven!" This time it's a deep masculine voice that sends butterflies loose in my belly. "Wait up," he says, reaching out and grabbing my hand.

Dad and I turn to face him. "Hey, Bash" I smile up at him.

"Thanks for coming," he says, his eyes only for me.

"Wouldn't be coming home without a Tigers game," I tell him.

"You headed home?" He glances over at my dad. "Good to see you, Tom."

"Yeah," I say, watching as my dad reaches out to shake his hand and they exchange pleasantries. It doesn't last long before Sebastian's eyes are once again locked with mine.

"You want to maybe grab something to eat?"

"I rode with Dad—" I start, and he stops me.

"I can take you home. Come on, Haven, for old times' sake."

"I thought we already did that?" I ask him.

"Yeah, but I thought we could catch up just us. Chloe is with Trina tonight."

"Go on, you deserve some fun," Dad encourages.

I'm nodding before I can get the words out. "Yeah, sure. I'd like that." It's not a lie, but hanging out with him with all of these old feelings swarming inside me. I'm not so sure it's a good idea, but I can't seem to make my mouth form the word 'no' when it comes to Sebastian.

"Great. I just need to say goodbye to my girl, and we can go."

"Okay, I'll uh, just wait here for you."

"No. You're coming with me." He reaches for my hand and addresses my father. "Good to see you again," he says to Dad, and then we're moving.

"All right, sweetheart, you be good for Mommy. I'll be there to get you tomorrow afternoon," he tells Chloe, taking her from her mom and kissing her cheek.

"Oh, I forgot I promised her a movie. Can I just bring her by your place after?" Trina asks him.

"Of course. I'll be there. Love you," he says, kissing his daughter's cheek.

"Bye, Daddy. Love you." He moves her back to Trina, and she surprises me when she leans over and reaches for me. "Miss Haven, I need a hug," she says, wiggling her little fingers.

Not one to tell her no, I take her in my arms and give her a big hug. "Remember to keep practicing your balance at home," I tell her.

"I will. Bye." She waves as I hand her back to Trina.

"She never stops." Trina laughs. "I'll see you guys later." No jealousy, no dirty looks. Just acceptance.

Sebastian waves to Chloe and blows her a kiss. Once they are out of sight, he turns his attention on me. "You ready?"

"Where are we going?"

"You'll see." He reaches for my hand again and leads me to his truck. "Have you heard anything about Mrs. Simone?" he asks me once we're on the road.

My hand tingles from his touch, and it's hard to not let it distract me. The feel of his skin against mine. It's been too long. "I talked to her earlier today. They want her off for three months. She's a diabetic, and it's taking longer for her bones to heal. They'll reassess then. They don't think she's going to need surgery. At least not right now."

"You staying on that long?" he asks, keeping his eyes on the road.

"Yeah, I told her I would stay. I have nothing pressing waiting for me back in New York." In fact, there is nothing at all waiting for me. Just an apartment that I'm rarely in because I spend so much time working.

He reaches across the console and entwines his fingers with mine. "Good. That gives me time."

"Time for what?"

"Time with you."

Biting down on my bottom lip, I fight to keep the tears at bay. Time with Sebastian sounds like the best plan I've ever heard. "I-I'd like that," I confess.

"Good. I wasn't planning on giving you a choice. I only get you for three months, and I plan to use my time wisely."

"Those are big promises," I murmur, but he still hears me.

"Not promises, Haven, facts." He pulls the truck into the lot of a local fast-food joint. "I thought we could go eat at the park like we used to."

"Is it still there?"

"Yep. Place looks the same. Although they do crack down on the parking these days." His deep chuckle fills the cab of the truck.

"I can't believe we never got caught."

"No way would I risk someone seeing you. I was always on the lookout."

"I'm glad you were. I was too lost in you to pay attention." The tension crackles between us.

"I remember. I was just as lost, but the need to keep you for my eyes only won over."

I want to cry. I want to let the hot tears that prick my eyes fall. I've missed him more than I let myself believe. I've missed home, this town, my parents. It's an emotional overload and to be spending this time with him has me second-guessing every decision I've ever made in my life.

"You want your usual?" he asks.

"Um... I haven't had a cheeseburger since I left for Juilliard."

"You're kidding me, right?" he asks.

"Nope."

"So... you want your usual?" he asks with a grin.

"Yes." I know it's going to take me forever to get back

into shape if I keep eating like this, but in a way, for the first time since I left for school, I'm living. Really taking the time to enjoy life and everything I've missed out on.

Sebastian growls when I offer to pay for mine, so I slide the money back into my purse and take the bag he hands me.

The drive to the park is quiet. "We have the place to ourselves," he says, pulling into the back of the lot and turning off his truck.

"Just like old times," I say before I can think better of it.

"The best of times."

"Here." I reach into the bag and hand him a straw for his drink, and then start laying our food out on the console between us. "Does Chloe get to be involved in every game?" I ask once our food is divided up.

"She does. Well, home games, at least. She doesn't get to come to all of the away games. It just depends on Trina and Dave's work schedule. They try to bring her to as many of them as they can."

"I love that. Tonight, I expected tension when you took me with you to say goodbye. There was none. The two of you really do have this co-parenting thing worked out."

"We're both happier apart. Our focus is on giving our daughter the love and support she needs."

"Oh, I guess I should tell you," I say, taking a drink of my Dr. Pepper. "Chloe kind of told Trina that I should love you so that you and I could get married."

"That girl—" He smiles, shaking his head. "—she's something else."

I expected him to be upset or be worried about Trina, but again, my assumptions were wrong. Maybe living in New York has me jaded. "She certainly is," I agree.

"So, tell me about you."

"You pretty much know my life. It's been plastered all over the papers."

"Not the gossip. You. Tell me about Juilliard and dancing and Broadway. What about your injury, are you better?"

"Juilliard was intense. Strict regimens, and lots of stuck-up snobs, if I'm being honest. Actually, that's pretty much how Broadway is too. As for my injury, I'm fine." I pause, deciding if I should tell him. "I'm not dancing. I haven't since the accident."

"What about the classes?" he asks.

"That's just showing the students. That's not even close to my eight- and ten-hour days practicing routines."

"Do you miss it?"

I take my time thinking about my answer. "No. I mean, I love to dance, and filling in for Mrs. Simone gives me that fix I need, but it's been nice to take a break and eat pizza and cheeseburgers for the first time in over fifteen years."

"It's really been that long?" he asks, surprise on his face.

"Yes. It's a constant battle to stay small, and I've basi-cally been on a never-ending diet for the last decade."

"Here." He hands me his half-eaten burger. "You've earned this."

"Stop." I laugh, pushing his hand away. "I'll be lucky to finish this one. When you eat salad and grilled chicken for the majority of your meals, this kind of food fills you up fast. Not to mention, I'm sure I'll be paying for it later."

"You should have told me."

"I wanted a burger." I shrug.

"Well, for what it's worth, I'm really glad you're home."

"Me too," I agree. "So, Miss Chloe, she's in preschool?"

"Yeah, she's going to be five in a few weeks. I swear she's five going on fifteen. She was so upset that her birthday missed the cut off to be enrolled in the big girl school. Her words, not mine."

"I remember those days... well, not when I was five, but I was so ready to be an adult. To graduate and forge my own path, and now here I am fifteen years later, and I'm up against a roadblock."

Silence surrounds us as we finish eating. Sebastian gathers our trash and hops out to throw it away. "Hey, what do you say, want me to push you on the swings?"

"Yes." I don't even hesitate as I climb out of his truck. "It's been years."

"Fifteen?" he asks.

"Yeah," I admit.

"Damn, I thought New York was this fun, exciting place, but you've been sheltered." He grabs hold of the swing. "Climb on." I waste no time doing as he asks. "Are you happy, Haven?" he asks from his place behind me. He gives me a push, and I begin to fly through the air. I lift my legs and tilt my head back, letting the wind hit my face.

"In this moment. Yes, I'm happy." It's easier to tell him the truth when my back is to him. I should have known better.

He stops the swing and leans in close. "In New York. Are you happy in New York?" he asks. His hot breath brushes across my cheek, causing goose bumps to break out on my skin.

"I- I don't know," I confess.

"Three months, right?" he asks.

"Three months?" I'm not sure what he's talking about.

"You're going to be here for three more months."

"Yes. At least that's the plan for now. As long as Mrs. Simone's recovery goes as planned."

He steps around me and bends so that we're eye to eye.

"That gives me time," he says, reaching out and pushing my hair out of my eyes.

"I know, for us to get to know each other again." I remind him of our earlier conversation.

"No, baby. That gives me three months to make you happy. To show you happiness again."

"Then what?" I ask, my voice barely audible.

"Then maybe, just maybe, you'll stay."

"You want me to stay?"

"More than anything."

My heart trips over in my chest and calls out his name. I thought time had dimmed the love I have for this man, but I was wrong. So very wrong. "Bash" I whisper.

"I've missed you, Haven. So much. I tried to make my marriage work for my daughter, but there was always something missing."

"You all seem good. Happy even," I comment.

He nods. "Yeah, that's about to get even better."

"Yeah?"

Another nod. "It's you, Haven. You're what was missing. I gave you my heart all those years ago, and it's still yours. Only now, you have to share it with a sassy soon-to-be five-year-old."

"That's—" I start, but he places his finger over my lips to stop me.

"Three months, Haven. I have three months to make you fall in love with me."

I want so badly to tell him that I love him now. That I never stopped. Fifteen years ago, this is the exact park where I told him I was going to Juilliard, and never looked back. Now that I've seen the grass on the other side of the world, it's not as green as I thought it would be.

His phone rings, and he sighs, pulling it out of his pocket. "I'm sorry. It's Trina," he says, accepting that call. "Hey, everything okay?" he asks, looking down at his phone.

"Daddy, I need to tell you goodnight." Chloe's sweet voice comes through the line. "Why's it dark? I can't see you."

"Sorry, baby. Daddy's at the park."

"The park? It's dark out."

"Miss Haven and I brought our food here to have dinner," he tells her honestly.

"Oh, is she there? Let me see," Chloe says excitedly.

He turns the phone to face me. "Hi, Chloe." I wave from my spot on the swings.

"Miss Haven, you like to swing? I love, love, *love* the swings. Daddy, when you get me tomorrow, can we take Miss Haven to swing?" she asks.

"Maybe not tomorrow, princess, but we will. I promise."

"Okay. Well, I need to go to sleep now. Night, Daddy, love you."

"I love you too, princess."

"Night, Miss Haven, oh, and don't forget to fall in love with my daddy."

I suck in a breath as Sebastian's laughter fills the night air.

"Well, she's consistent. I'll give her that," he says, ending the call.

"We're confusing her."

"No. She's a smart little girl."

"We should probably get going. It's getting late."

Disappointment crosses his face, but I hold strong. A lot of things were said tonight, things that cause my heart to race. Then there's Chloe and her declaration. How easy it would be to tell her that she doesn't have to worry about me falling in love with her daddy because I never stopped loving him. However, I don't think that's the right thing to say. I live in New York, and even though we've revisited our past, that's not our future... is it?

CHAPTER 5

Sebastian

I finish mowing the back lawn and push the mower to the front. As I pass the porch, I grab the bottle of water off the railing and chug it. It's a gorgeous late-September Saturday, one with the sun high in the sky and a light breeze out of the east. I spent the morning at the weight room with the team, but now have the rest of the day to myself. A perfect day to get a little yard work done before Chloe arrives.

Memories of spending last night with Haven filter through my mind as I wipe my forehead with my T-shirt. Everything from the drive-through food to eating in the park, swinging in the same place we did all those years ago, and video chatting with my daughter before bedtime. It was the perfect ending to a great Friday night, all capped off by a peck on the cheek after I walked her to her parents' front door and bid her goodnight.

Oh, I wanted more than just a chaste kiss at the end of our time together, but with Haven, it's a marathon, not a race. Slow and steady. That's how I'll win in my quest for her heart.

It's funny how my own heart knew it was her it was missing. Like when she left, she took a piece with her, and now that she's back, it's whole again. Maybe I shouldn't have laid all my cards on the table so quickly, but you know what? Fuck it. I want her. More today than ever before. I could tell by the look in her eyes she's not happy in New York. Even before she confirmed it, I saw it written in her delicate features, in those emerald eyes.

Then, she confirmed it, and it was like someone blew the whistle.

Game. On.

I've tried to play it cool today. I don't want to bombard her with texts and phone calls, even though I'd love nothing more than to hear her voice or see her pretty face on my phone screen. Instead, to occupy my time, I've washed two loads of laundry, some dishes, and have been outside working in the yard since noon. The shrubs are trimmed, weeds pulled in the rock beds, and the gravel graded in the driveway to refill those pesky holes. And now, I'm finishing the yard.

I polish off the bottle of water and toss it in the trash can. With one more wipe across my face, I take off the shirt, using it to dry the back of my neck, and throw it on the closest Adirondack chair. I don't usually run around without a shirt on, but I'm baking under the sun and tired of the shirt sticking to my back.

I make my way up front and line the push mower up along the sidewalk. With one pull, it fires to life and I start my first pass. As I head back a second time, I spy a woman jogging down the street. First thing I notice is her outfit—

tight gray shorts that accentuate lean, muscular legs, and a red sports bra. My dick actually twitches.

But what catches my attention next is the long, curly hair pulled high on her head. I know that hair. I've run my fingers through it more times than I can count and can practically smell the sweet, fruity scent of her shampoo. It's probably my favorite of all fragrances.

Haven seems to startle when her eyes meet mine. Even through sunglasses, I can see the wide whites of her eyes. She stops running and walks over as I release the handle on the mower, shutting it down.

"This is where you live?" she asks, taking in the small but neat house behind me.

"This is it," I confirm, letting my eyes roam over her body once more. It's even more spectacular now that she's standing directly in front of me.

"I remember when the Johnsons lived here," she says.

"They both passed in the last five years. I bought this place a couple of years back from their daughter, Regina."

She smiles off in the distance as she takes in the blue front door and white-painted porch. When she glances back this way, I notice, even behind her shades, it's not my face she's focused on. Her eyes are glued to my chest. My very shirtless chest. I follow her line of sight and see a few blades of grass stuck to my skin.

"So," I start, a smile spreading across my face when she doesn't even acknowledge I said anything. She just continues to openly gape at me, something that actually makes me preen like a peacock. "Did you know aliens landed on the football field this morning?"

Haven makes a noise in response but must not be listening.

So, I continue.

"Yeah, once they disembarked their spaceship, they started beaming people up left and right. I heard Principal Edwards was taken and has probably already been probed," I state with a straight face, my arms crossing over my chest.

Her eyes flare before meeting mine. "That's interesting."

"Isn't it? I'm not sure if they probe everyone or just the really smart ones. Who knows with aliens like that."

Her eyes widen in shock and her sweet little mouth falls open. "Wait, what?"

Finally, I bust out laughing, shaking my head at her confusion. "You were totally ogling my chest."

Her cheeks turn pink as she opens her mouth, stammering, "W-What? I did no such thing. I was looking at your house, the basket you have... hanging," she insists, waving her hands toward my porch.

"If that basket was on my chest maybe," I tease, secretly loving the fact she couldn't stop looking at my body.

"I... no, it..." she sighs deeply. "Fine, I was totally checking you out. I'm so sorry," she insists, covering her eyes with her hands. Her embarrassment is adorable.

"Hey," I start, reaching up and moving her hands, "it's fine. Actually, I rather enjoyed it," I say with a wink.

"Well, who can blame me? I mean, you're practically out here naked, Bash, I bet every neighbor within a one-block radius of your yard is peeking through their windows right now," she sasses, placing her hands on her hips.

"I'm half-naked? Oh, no, sweetheart. You're out here, *in public*, in a bra and those tight shorts that make your ass look fantastic. If anyone is doing any peeking right now, it's the men," I argue.

"It's hot!" she insists.

"Yes, it is. Hence, the lack of a shirt."

Her eyes fall down once more, but her gaze only lasts a few seconds. "Well, the years have been good to you, Bash."

"And you as well, Have."

Electricity starts to crackle around us, zipping through the thick air and pulsing through my veins. It's almost hard to breathe when she's standing in front of me, and no, I'm not talking about the heat of the day. I'm referring to that same sexual desire that's always swirling around us and apparently is showing no signs of ebbing, even fifteen years later.

I wonder if she feels it too.

"Did you run all the way into town?" I ask, trying to get my brain away from dangerous territory involving her current state of dress.

"Yeah, I used to run on a treadmill with my trainer but haven't really done much of it since I've been home. I thought it'd be a good idea to burn off that burger from last night," she says with a grin.

A quick scan of her body confirms she can afford to eat a few more cheeseburgers without it affecting her whatsoever, but I keep that to myself. "How are your parents? It was good to see your dad last night at the game. I've seen them around town some, but not too much. I guess they don't take in Tigers football games too much."

"No, probably not much anymore. They stay close to home a lot, especially during the heavy harvest seasons," she says, referring to the farm her parents own just outside town. They have everything from sweet corn, strawberries, and blueberries, and about every kind of garden vegetable known to man. Plus, they have animals, which takes up a lot of their time.

"You know, I'd love to bring Chloe out sometime to see

the animals. She has this thing for chickens," I tell her, a little hopeful she'll invite me out.

Fortunately, I don't have to beg because she replies, "Any time. Mom and Dad would love to show her around and let her pet the animals."

Smiling, I nod, wondering how quickly I can work that out. Chloe will be here later, and she's mine until she goes to school Monday. Maybe we can go for a visit someday soon. Or...

"You have plans later?"

She exhales. "Well, not really. I promised Mom I'd help her clean out the storage room. It's packed with totes of craft stuff, and I'm definitely not looking forward to that," she says with a sigh.

I remember her mom knitting things all winter long back when we were in school, including blankets for local nursing homes and hospitals. Haven used to always say there was enough yarn and other supplies in the craft room to outfit a small country during the worst of winters. I peeked in there one time and it was packed full of stuff. I can't imagine having to go through that room now.

"Well, if you'd like an excuse to get out of sorting yarn, I'd love to have you for dinner tonight. Chloe will be here by then, and as long as you don't mind mac and cheese as a side, we'd love to have you."

Haven's moan is almost orgasmic. At least, that's what my cock thinks because it starts to thicken in my shorts. "Mac and cheese? Are you kidding me? I haven't had that in forever. I'm going to gain a hundred pounds if I keep hanging out with you," she teases, referring to all the foods she, apparently, hasn't eaten since she was here.

My eyes go ahead and take a leisurely perusal of her body. She's defined, but not in a too-muscular way. She takes care of her body as a dancer, and that includes watching what she eats. I linger a little too long on her chest, and when my eyes finally make their way back up to her face, I give her a slow, wolfish grin. "Sweetheart, you could gain a hundred pounds and still look fucking amazing."

Her cheeks blush from the compliment, and her eyes avert for just a few seconds. "Well, you're quite the charmer, aren't you?"

"I call it like I see it," I answer.

She seems to think for a few seconds, and I really hope it's about the dinner invitation. I wasn't planning on dinner for three tonight, but I can make adjustments. I've always got meat in the freezer from the local meat locker, and it would be nothing to take a couple of steaks or even some chicken out to thaw.

"How about five? That gives me a few hours to go home, help Mom, and shower."

"Five is perfect."

"Do you want me to bring anything?" she asks.

"Just yourself and an appetite."

Haven smiles. "Okay. I'll see you at five?"

"I'll be here," I reply, my own smile matching hers.

"Well, I better get back," she says, pointing down the road with her thumb.

"Be careful, Have," I state as she starts to jog away.

I wish I could say I pull the starter and fire up the mower, but that'd be a lie. I stand here and watch her go, observing the way her legs carry her away. She has an athletic physique that seems to push all of my buttons, in a good way.

Eventually, after she's rounded the corner and is out of sight, I pull the cord to finish trimming the grass. I even pretend like I don't realize I do it with a smile on my face.

* * *

"Can I play with chalk?" Chloe asks from the back door as I fire up the grill. It's almost five and I'm starting to get a little anxious to see Haven. She should be here any moment, and I haven't told my daughter her ballet teacher is coming yet. I thought it would be a fun surprise for her.

After I finished the yard, I picked up the living room and kitchen, as well as ran the vacuum and dusted the end tables. The place wasn't super messy, mostly because my little tornado of a daughter hasn't been here for a few days, but I want to make a good impression on Haven.

When Trina brought Chloe home, after seeing a matinee Disney movie in the theatre, she instantly started getting all of her "things" out. Without her noticing, I've been successfully walking behind her and picking it back up. Now, she wants to play outside for a bit, which means she isn't messing up the inside. I'll take it.

"That's fine, sweetie. You have to stay in the back here and draw on the sidewalk, okay?"

"Okay, Daddy. I won't go up front," she insists, heading back inside to retrieve the tote full of sidewalk chalks of all sizes and colors.

I keep an eye on her as the grill warms up. She's on her third rainbow when I hear a car pull into the driveway and stop, quickly followed by a car door shutting. My heart rate kicks up a bit as anticipation fills my body. I don't say anything to Chloe as I walk over to the edge of the deck and glance down the driveway. There she is, all beautiful and fresh from a shower. When she sees me, she softly grins and heads my way.

"Hey," I say as she reaches the back deck.

"Hi."

Chloe suddenly realizes we have company and jumps up, throwing her arms around Haven's waist. "Miss Haven! Did you come to draw rainbows with me?"

Haven doesn't miss a beat. Her smile broadens as she replies, "I sure did."

She throws me a wink before heading over to where my daughter has been drawing on the sidewalk. Together, they sit down and draw everything from rainbows to fish to a princess crown. All I can do is stare at their easy interaction. Haven is patient and encouraging, in that maternal way any single father would appreciate. But since it's her—*my* Haven—it just means that much more.

"Hope you're okay with chicken drumsticks," I say as I scrape the grill grates with my brush.

"They're my favorite!" Chloe chimes in. "And mac and cheese."

"But not the box stuff, right?" I ask, already smiling.

"Nope! We makedid our own." My daughter looks over at Haven, and without missing a beat, adds, "Sometimes my mommy makes the boxed cheese. It doesn't taste as good, but I tell her I like it."

Haven turns to me and grins. I shrug. "What can I say? No Kraft stuff in this house." I place the drumsticks on the grill and lightly season them before closing the lid and heading down the steps. When I reach the base of the stairs, Haven glances up with a big grin as my daughter colors a big yellow circle. "Is that the sun?"

Chloe glances up, a look of offense on her sweet little face. "It's a chicken, Daddy."

"Oh." When she adds the feet and head, it finally starts to resemble a chicken.

"You like chickens, huh?" Haven asks, watching my daughter draw.

"They're my favorite. Like mac and cheese."

"Have you ever seen a chicken up close?"

Chloe turns all of her attention to her drawing partner and shakes her head. "No, but I want my own chickens, and then I see them real close. Right, Daddy?"

"Right, sweetie," I reply with a smile.

Haven glances over her shoulder at me, as if seeking permission. When I give her a slight nod, she gives my daughter the best gift she could. "Would you like to come over and see my parents' chickens someday?"

"Today?" Chloe asks, her eyes wide with shock.

"No, not today, but maybe soon. My parents have animals and they have about two dozen chickens," Haven replies.

"Is that like a million?"

With a snicker, Haven answers, "No, it's twenty-four. If we go out in the morning, you can help collect eggs."

Chloe jumps up and runs straight for me, her little legs carrying her up the stairs as fast as they can. "Daddy, Daddy, can we go see the chickens and get the eggs?"

I squat down, meeting her eager face. "If you'd like, I'm sure we can arrange this soon."

"Today?"

"No."

"Tomorrow?" Her eyes plead with me.

I glance down at Haven, who's already grinning from ear to ear. "Maybe," I answer, not really comfortable with just inviting ourselves out to the Deckers' farm without their consent.

"Yay!"

"I said maybe."

She throws her arms around my neck and kisses my

scruffy cheek. "That means yes," she whispers, making me laugh.

"I have an idea. While I cook the chicken, maybe you and Miss Haven can get the mac and cheese ready?"

"Yes! I'll show her how to put the extra cheese inside to make it extra gooder."

"I do love extra cheese," Haven says, joining us on the deck.

"Come on, Miss Haven. Let's go make the cheese."

My daughter leads her inside the house, chatting about the chickens the whole way. I grab the tongs and flip the legs, doing everything and anything to get my mind off the fact Haven Decker is inside my house right now, cooking with my daughter. It's a little mind-blowing, honestly. A week ago, I never would have thought she'd be back in Hope, let alone standing in my kitchen. But here we are, doing something as mundane and domesticated as cooking dinner together.

It feels really fucking good.

After dinner, Chloe draws Haven into the living room to do a few stretches and to work on balance. Haven said it probably wasn't best to do it after dinner, but my daughter, the fierce warrior, wasn't to be deterred. I'm standing in the kitchen, cleaning up the plates and listening to them laugh and carry on. Even though I'm not standing in the other room, watching, I can hear Haven give polite instructions and can tell my daughter is following them. Haven even praises Chloe after a job well done.

When the dishes are drying, I toss the towel on the counter and head to the doorway between the living room and the kitchen. Both of them are balanced on their left foot, their right leg drawn up like a flamingo, and their arms poised over their heads.

"Daddy, look. I can balance good."

"You're doing wonderful, sweetheart, but it's probably time to relax and get in the tub. You have half the backyard on your legs still," I tell her, referring to the mixture of dirt, grass, and chalk on her little legs.

"Do I gots to?"

"Yes, Chloe, you gots to."

My daughter turns and looks up at her ballet teacher. "Will you be here when I get done?"

She opens her mouth, not really sure how to respond. "I can stay for a little bit longer."

"I'll take a really fast bath!" she responds, darting down the hall like a bullet.

I chuckle. "That means she's not going to wash her hair." I point in the direction my daughter just went. "I'm going to get her bath started and I'll be right out. Make yourself comfortable."

I dart down the hall and into the bathroom. I turn on the water to the temperature Chloe likes and add a few bubbles. I grab a towel and a washcloth from the cabinet and set them on the toilet. Chloe comes in, already stripped down, and jumps in the water. I soap-up the washcloth and set it aside. "I'll be back in ten minutes. You can play for a little bit and then we'll wash your hair."

"Okay," she sings, covering herself in bubbles.

I shut off the water before slipping out, making sure to leave the door open so I can hear her. Haven is still in the living room, taking in a small grouping of picture frames on the wall. There's a photo of me holding Chloe for the first time in the hospital, one of her first day of preschool, a few of us at football games last fall, and a handful of candids from activities we've done together.

"She seems like a happy little girl," Haven says the moment I step into the room.

"She is. Admittedly, in the beginning, it wasn't always easy between Trina and me, but we've always strived to do what is needed for Chloe. She's always first."

Those sexy green eyes turn and lock on me. "You're an amazing dad, Bash."

I actually feel a blush creep up my neck. "Thanks," I reply, trying to avert my eyes. Only, when I do, they land on her lips. Her very plump, perfectly ripe lips. The ones I used to get lost in for hours at a time, kissing her until they were chapped, and I was so fucking horny, I couldn't even see straight.

She turns until we're facing each other. I take a step closer, her familiar scent drawing me in like a moth to a flame. I don't know who moves first, her or me, but her arms go to my shoulders, while mine wrap around her waist. We're a breath apart when she licks her lips in invitation. My mind tries to tell me this probably isn't the brightest idea, but my body strongly disagrees.

"Why haven't you kissed me yet?" she whispers, gazing up at me with a mix of desire and challenge.

"I was trying to be polite." Why is it so hard to breathe when she's in my arms?

A coy grin slips across those very lips. "Personally, I really like it when your manners are thrown out the window." She's like gasoline to an already burning blaze.

I chuckle. "I'd really like nothing more than to kiss you right now, Have, but I'm afraid I won't be able to stop. I want you so badly." My words come out a whisper.

"I want you too," she replies, her fingers tightening into my shoulders as she presses her chest to my own, as if daring me to do it anyway.

"I can't do anything more than kiss you tonight, Have. Not with my daughter here."

"I understand," Haven responds, her chin jutting up in dare. "You know," she says, running her hand down the front of my chest, "your daughter isn't *here* right now."

And that's all it takes. My lips crash into hers in a frenzy of pent-up lust and age-old desire. It's like a homecoming as she opens her mouth and my tongue delves inside, tasting her for the first time. Her nails bite into my shirt as she presses herself further into my chest, as if she can't get close enough. My cock is pulsing in my shorts, begging to be let out to play, and as much as I try to ignore him, he still lets his presence be known the moment Haven presses her body into it.

This.

This is what life's been missing.

This wild, crazy, can't-be-contained desire.

I've always had it for Haven and am happy to know the feeling's only been in hibernation for the last decade or so.

"Daddy! Some of the water flew out of the tub by itself!"

My lips rip from Haven's, our breathing labored, as reality settles in.

Our kiss has come to an end.

CHAPTER 6

Haven

It's been two days since I've seen Sebastian, and I can still feel his lips pressed to mine. It's as if no time has passed between us. Except years have passed, and he has an adorable little girl to show for it. I can't stop the giggle that escapes my lips as I think about her words about the water flying out of the tub by itself. She's such a great kid, and it's obvious that Sebastian and Trina are doing an amazing job raising her.

Glancing at the clock, I see it's time for my littles to be arriving for my next class any minute. That means I get to see him. Get to see them. He texted me earlier and asked if we could have dinner after class. Of course I said yes. I would be a fool not to. More time with both of them is exactly what I need. I've really missed them these last couple of days.

"Miss Haven!" I hear Chloe's sweet voice. I turn just in time for her to launch herself at me, wrapping her little arms around my waist as best as she can. "Daddy said we get to go get pizza after class," she tells me excitedly.

"Daddy said no such thing," Sebastian's deep voice announces. "Hey, Have." He leans in and presses his lips to my cheek before turning his attention back to his daughter. "What I said was that we were going to have dinner with Haven tonight."

"Yeah, pizza," Chloe says, like it's the only option.

"We took her for pizza last time. Why don't we pick something else?"

I watch in amusement as Chloe taps her chin with her index finger deep in thought. "Oh!" Her eyes light up. "Can we go to that chicken place, you know the one that only lets us have chicken and French fries?" she asks, hopeful.

Sebastian glances at me for approval. "I don't care where we eat as long as I get to sit beside you," I say, bopping her on the nose. She offers me a toothy grin.

"See, Daddy, pizza!" Chloe cheers, rushing off to greet some of her friends who have started to arrive for class.

"You can't let her get her way all the time," he tells me, stepping closer.

"I like pizza," I say, gazing up at him.

"I like you."

"Yeah? Does that earn me a kiss later?"

"Later? Why not now?"

"Your fan club just showed up." I glance behind him at the moms who are watching us with interest.

"Even more reason to do it now," he says, leaning in and pressing his lips to mine before I can object.

He pulls away, leaving me dazed, and it was just a quick peck. "You're going to start rumors," I say, taking a step away from him. It's not that I don't want to be next to him.

In fact, there is nowhere else I'd rather be, but I need to remember that I have to remain professional.

"What rumors? That I'm kissing my girlfriend, hello?"

My heart thunders in my chest. "Is that what I am?"

His hand finds its way to my cheek. "No, Haven. You're more than that. So much more, but we're going to start there."

"I'm Chloe's teacher."

He nods. "And she adores you. I'm not hiding this from anyone, especially not my daughter, and not the nosy-ass dance moms who stare at me like I'm some piece of meat."

I let my eyes rake over his body. "I can't say as I blame them," I comment, my eyes meeting his once again.

"Keep looking at me like that, Have, and we're going to be locking ourselves in your office."

"Is that a threat or a promise? I just need to figure out which route I'm going to take," I ask.

"Both, beautiful. It's both." He leans in for another kiss, which has the girls screaming that we now have cooties. "I'll be watching." He winks and saunters off to the edge of the room to take his seat next to the horny dance moms. I watch as they all stare at him curiously, and then they pounce. I can't make out what they're asking, but I'm certain from the grin he's wearing, he's getting badgered with questions about us.

"All right, ladies. Are we ready to get started?" I ask the class. A chorus of "yeses" ring out as they scramble to get into position.

Over the thirty minutes, we practice poses and balance. At this age, it's really the very basics and ensuring that they're having fun. That's what Mrs. Simone did for me when I was Chloe's age. She made dancing entertaining. That's when I fell in love with it. At five years old, I knew that I wanted to dance. Then, I fell in love with Sebastian. The day I walked away from us will forever be one of the greatest regrets of my life. I thought I needed dancing and Broadway to be happy. Little did I know a trip home and a few stolen kisses would prove to me otherwise.

"You ladies did fantastic!" I praise the class, clapping my hands together. "I can tell you've been working hard at home." A sea of little heads nod up and down, giving me an array of toothless grins for the praise.

"Miss Haven, is it time for pizza?" Chloe calls out.

"You bet," I assure her. "I'll see you all next week. Remember, practice your balance." It's something I tell them every class. Most of them are still clumsy and finding their footing. Practice will keep them active and only improve their movements with time.

"Miss Haven."

I feel a tug on my too-big T-shirt. Looking down, I see Lucy. She's one of the shyest kids in the class. I kneel down to her level. "What can I do for you, Lucy?"

"I'm pwacticing weally hawd," she whispers.

"That's great. I'm so proud of you."

"I's still fall awot." Her voice is sullen, and the sadness on her face pulls at my heartstrings.

"Oh, Lucy, we all fall, sweetheart. That's why we come to class. We have to practice to learn."

"I wanna be wike you when I get big," she says, her big brown eyes staring at me in adoration.

I can't resist pulling her into a hug. "You can be anything you want to be. You have to work hard and never give up." That earns me a hug, her little arms wrapping around my neck.

"Thank you." Her mother smiles fondly. She's one of

the few who don't hit on Sebastian when he's here. I like her on that alone.

"You're welcome. Lucy, I'll see you next class." She gives me a smile that washes away the sadness from just minutes before. I take the next ten minutes, passing out hugs and waves of goodbyes. It doesn't slip my notice that my smile is wide and genuine. It's been years since I've been this relaxed and happy. I think the last time was when I was here, when I was home with Sebastian.

"Finally," Sebastian says, wrapping his arm around my waist. "I didn't think they would ever leave."

"Hey." I smack at his chest. "Those are my students you're talking about."

"Your students?" He raises his eyebrows.

"They're mine for now," I explain. I don't tell him that with each passing day, I want this to be my life. Everything I ever thought that I wanted isn't what I want at all. It took coming home for me to finally admit that to myself. I have a lot of decisions to make about my future.

"Pizza!" Chloe cheers.

"Come on, Chloe, let's do something else."

"Aw, Dad," she whines.

"Pizza is fine with me. But I have an idea." I motion my index finger for Chloe to come closer. Bending down to her level, I whisper in her ear, "What if we take it to the park?"

"Oh, yes!" She jumps up and down in excitement.

"What are you two scheming?" Sebastian laughs.

Chloe looks at me for permission, and I nod. "The park! Miss Haven says we can eat the pizza at the park."

"Good idea. Fresh air and she can run off some of that energy that seems to always be dancing on the balls of her feet."

"I was the same way. Even as a teenager."

"I remember," he says, his eyes softening.

"Come on." Chloe grabs each of our hands and begins to pull us toward the door.

"Hold on, let me grab my things and lock up." I rush to the small office, gather my things, and hit the lights, before meeting them at the front door.

"To have an ounce of her energy." I laugh as Chloe runs from one swing to the next at the park. I'm not sure why she needs to switch every few minutes. They all look the same to me.

"You and me both," Sebastian agrees as his phone rings. He glances at the screen. "Sorry, this is Trina," he says, placing the phone to his ear. "Hey, Trina." He listens and nods even though she can't see him. "Sure, that's not a problem. We just had dinner at the park. I'll drop her off on my way home. Okay. Bye." He ends the call, setting his phone on the picnic table between us.

"Everything okay?"

"Yeah. That was Trina. Her sister, Tracy, has extra passes for the zoo tomorrow. Since there's no preschool and Trina is off, she wanted to take Chloe."

"She's going to love that."

"Yeah." He nods, smiling at his daughter.

"You guys do that a lot? Change the routine?"

"Pretty much." He laughs. "Trina's schedule is crazy, and we adjust as needed. It's nice that we're in the same town and school district."

"I'm in awe of the two of you and the ease that you raise Chloe. It's truly amazing how well you get along."

"We tried, you know? We wanted it to work for Chloe, but we're both happier apart. She's going to forever connect us, and I will always care about her, but that's where it ends."

"Miss Haven!" Chloe calls out. "Watch me."

"I'm watching!" I call back as she climbs the ladder for the slide. She sits at the top, pushes herself, and throws her hands up in the air, laughing all the way down. "Great job." I clap for her, and her smile is huge as she races to the steps to repeat the process.

"She adores you."

"Just her?" I ask before I can stop the words from leaving my lips.

"No. Not just her. Her daddy adores you too." He reaches over and entwines his fingers with mine. "He always has." His lips find their way to my temple.

For the life of me, I don't know how I was able to walk away from him all those years ago. I'm struggling to leave this park. I want to be where he is. "You're not so bad," I say, trying to lighten the mood.

"Hey, Chloe, it's time to go," he calls out. His voice lowers just for me. "I'll show you not bad. Come back to my place."

"Okay." I don't bother to play hard to get. He's caught me. Hook, line, and sinker. I'd follow him anywhere.

"Here." Reaching into his pocket, he retrieves his keys. "Go ahead and head to my place. I'll drop Chloe off and meet you there."

"Does she need anything from your place?"

"Nah, we keep clothes for her at both of our places. Make yourself at home. I'll be there soon."

"Do we hafta go, Daddy?" Chloe asks.

"We do. Mommy called, and she and Aunt Tracy are

going to take you and your cousins to the zoo tomorrow, so
I'm taking you back to Mommy's house."

"The zoo! Come on, Daddy, we gots to go." She grabs
his hand, causing us both to throw our heads back in
laughter.

"Give Haven a hug," he tells her.

"Bye, Miss Haven." Her arms wrap around me, and I
hug her back.

"Have fun tomorrow. I can't wait to hear all about it."
I'm not just saying the words. I really can't wait to hear
about her day at the zoo—living it through her excited eyes.

"Come on, Daddy." She tugs at Sebastian's hand.

"I'll be home soon, baby. Drive safe," he says, allowing
Chloe to pull him to his truck.

I sit here on the picnic table and watch them drive
away. All I can think about is the sound of him saying he's
coming home to me. I want that. I want him. I want Chloe
and all of her infectious energy. I want every facet of my life
wrapped up in theirs.

* * *

His house is quiet, too quiet without Chloe's chatter. That
little girl has quickly found her way into my heart. "Just like
her daddy," I murmur. After setting my keys on the table
next to the front door, I make my way into the kitchen.
There are a few dishes in the sink, so I decide to wash them.
Sebastian is a single father. Sure, he and Trina co-parent,
but when he has Chloe, it's just him. I like to think even
something as small as cleaning up his kitchen will save him
some time and give him more time with his daughter.
Tonight, it gives me his time, and there is nothing I want
more.

After wrapping up with the dishes, I pick up the living room, and I'm ready to go on the hunt for the sweeper when he walks in the door. I watch as he makes it a point to turn the lock before walking my way. "You picked up. You didn't have to do that."

"I was here and had some time on my hands."

"Thank you." He leans down and kisses me, soft and slow. "Come with me." With my hand in his, he leads me to the kitchen, where he sees that I cleaned that too. "You didn't have to do all this," he says, gesturing with his free hand to the now clean kitchen.

"I know, but I plan on taking up all of your spare time tonight, so in my eyes, it's an even trade."

"You want my time, huh?" he asks, his eyes light.

"I want you."

A low growl from deep in his throat passes his lips. He hits the light switch, bathing us in darkness. With his hand clasped tightly around mine, I follow him as he turns off the rest of the lights and leads me down the hall to his room.

As soon as we enter his room, his hands are gripping my ass and lifting me. Instinctively, I wrap my legs around his waist, fusing my lips to his. He turns, pressing my back against the door. His lips, hot and wet, devour mine. I bury my hands in his hair and take every swipe of his tongue that he's willing to give me.

"Bash" I moan when his lips trail down my neck.

"Too fucking long, Have. It's been too fucking long since I've had you in my arms." His grip on my ass grows tighter, almost painful, but his lips on my neck are enough to distract me from the bite of his fingertips on my flesh.

"Please," I beg. I can't ever remember a time when I was so desperate for a man's touch.

My plea sends him into action as he pulls away from the

wall, carrying me to the bed. He releases his hold on me, placing me on the soft mattress. "I need you naked, Haven." His voice is gravelly. "Now."

I spring into action and pull my oversized T-shirt over my head, tossing it on the floor. In the shadows of the room, I watch as he takes two steps back and reaches for the hem of his T-shirt, pulling it off and tossing it on the floor. Sliding to the edge of the bed, I stand on wobbly legs and remove my leggings and panties all in one action, kicking them to the side once they reach my ankles. Standing to my full height, I manage to wrangle myself out of my sports bra and toss it as well.

My chest is rapidly rising and falling with each staggered breath. I watch with rapt attention, pulling air into my lungs as he strips out of his jeans and boxer briefs, all in one go, just as I did seconds before. He's standing naked in front of me for the first time in years.

Sebastian.

My Sebastian.

The man I love.

The man I have always loved.

"I don't know where to start," he murmurs, his voice thick. "I never thought we'd be here again, Haven. I thought I'd lost you forever, and now here you are. I—" He starts and stops.

"You what?"

"I want to devour you. I want my hands and my lips on every single fucking inch of your skin. I want to brand you with my touch, so no man other than me will ever be able to satisfy you." My body quivers at his confession.

"You did that, Bash. Fifteen years ago, you were that man, and you're still that man today." I take a step toward him. He stands still, not moving a muscle. "I left you, I left us, and I'm so sorry for that. I know now it was a mistake. It was always meant to be us."

"I feel it here." He places his hand over his heart.

I take another step, bringing us toe to toe. Reaching for his hand, I place it against my bare chest, over my heart. "Here," I whisper.

"You're leaving, Haven, and I don't know that I can handle watching you walk away from me again. I live here. My life is here with Chloe."

I can hear the anguish in his voice and feel the crack in my heart at the mere thought of ever walking away from him again. "I guess you missed the headline, then?"

"What headline?"

"The one that reported why I came back after all these years."

"You lost me, baby. What are you talking about?"

I wrap my arms around him, holding him close. My naked breasts press against his bare chest, and his hard length is prominent against my belly. "I came home to you."

"What are you saying, Haven?"

"I'm saying I want you."

"Haven," he growls.

"Later. We can discuss it later. Right now, I need you to remind me how it feels with you to be inside me."

"Fuck."

Pulling out of his arms, I let my shaking legs carry me back to the bed. Sliding into the center, I lie here, waiting for him. My heart is pounding in my chest, not because I'm scared or worried. No, it's the anticipation of being with him again. "Bash!" I call out for him.

I feel the bed dip and the heat of his body as he settles between my thighs. The sound of a condom wrapper tearing pierces through the silence of the room, and suddenly he's there. His hands are braced on either side of my head.

"Haven, I wanted to take my time with you. I wanted to explore this sexy body of yours, but you've got me so worked up, I'm going to have to do that later. Right now, I need to remind you. To remind both of us." With that, he pushes forward and doesn't stop until he's buried deep inside me. Where he belongs.

His lips find mine, and as his hips begin to thrust, his tongue invades my mouth, giving me every part of him. My legs wrap around his waist, and my hands slide under his arms, allowing my fingers to dig into his back. "More, Bash. I need more."

"Home," he whispers against my lips as his thrusts grow faster, more frantic as he pistons in and out of me. "Your pussy is like a vise around my cock," he murmurs, his lips next to my ear.

"It's... been a while," I pant.

"Not here," he says on a growl. "We don't talk about that here, in my bed, when I'm buried balls deep inside you."

"Just you," I tell him, trying to soothe his ruffled feathers. I don't tell him that Chloe is a reminder to me every day that he was with someone else, married to someone else. My fault that I left, but I'm back, and I want them both. I want to spend the rest of my life with him. I want to help him raise his daughter, and with any luck, we'll be blessed with a few more of our own. I want it all with him. I can see our future just as clear as I could all those years ago, until I got the letter from Juilliard. This time, I'm not a young girl with big dreams of the spotlight. This time I'm a woman who just found the missing piece of her soul wrapped up in the only man she's ever loved.

"Hey." He stills. "Where did you go?"

New York. "I'm right here," I assure him.

"This moment changes things, Haven."

"I know." I nod.

"I won't let you go again. Not without a fight." I can hear the conviction in his voice. He means what he says.

"I'm not going anywhere." Just like that, the decisions I needed to make for my future are clearly written before me. This is my home. Here in Hope, Idaho. The small town I grew up in, and the first man to ever have access to my body will now be the last. This is what I want out of life. Not the grueling sixteen-hour days, the backstabbing, the feeling of constantly having to watch over your shoulder. No, I want giggles from little girls, dinner at the park, and I want to make love to the man who owns every single piece of me.

"I-I can't hold off much longer," he grits out. "Fuck, you feel incredible."

"Faster," I pant, as I feel my spine start to tingle. I'm close to euphoria that only Sebastian can bring me. It's only ever been him. His pace quickens, and so does my grip on his back as my nails dig deep. "Sebastian!" I cry out his name as waves of pleasure roll through my body like liquid fire.

His hips jerk once, twice, three times until he too is calling out my name as he loses control, releasing inside me. Spent, he rests his forehead against mine. We're both panting, trying to suck much-needed air into our lungs.

"I love you, Haven." His lips press against mine.

My breath falters as I let his words sink in. Staring up at him, I know that I feel the same way. It's always been him. "I love you too," I reply as he pulls out and stands.

"Come on, baby. We need a shower."

I don't argue as I allow him to help me from the bed. I'm

relaxed and zoned out. All I want to do is curl up in his arms and sleep. Little did I know that's exactly what he had planned. We take the fastest shower ever, before sliding back into his bed, naked and with still-wet hair, and burrow under the covers.

"This is what I've been missing. It's always been you," he murmurs, kissing the top of my head.

"I'm home." No truer words have ever been spoken. It's not Hope, Idaho, that has me feeling at home. No, it's the man with his arms wrapped around me in a cocoon. It's his adorable little girl who also owns a piece of my heart. Wherever they are is where I want to be.

This is my life.

They are my future.

CHAPTER 7

Sebastian

Best night of sleep I've had in ages.

Waking with Haven in my arms before the sun even rose was like heaven. My cock thought so also and was all too eager for a repeat of last night's activities. So I indulged once more until we were both panting and exhausted, sated and happy.

Now, the sun is up and so am I. I have to leave for work in less than an hour, and I want to feed Haven before I go. She's still curled up in my bed, her naked body tangled in my sheets. The view is pretty fucking spectacular. It's why I'm still wearing a smile as I flip the second batch of pancakes.

"Something smells amazing," Haven says through a yawn.

When I turn around, she's wearing one of my Hope High football T-shirts. The view is even better than seeing her in my bed, because now she's in my clothes. And now my cock is completely hard and ready to play.

"You didn't have to get up. I was going to bring it to you," I tell her, trying to ignore how fucking amazing her bare legs look so I don't scorch the food.

"Breakfast in bed?" she asks, coming up behind me and wrapping her arms around my chest. "I don't recall seeing this side of you way back when."

"That's because we were both living at home, eating the food our parents bought. It was hard enough taking you on dates and finding places to hide on deserted country roads to have my wicked way with you in the back seat."

She giggles. "Those were the days."

I remove the pancakes from the griddle and flip off the burner before turning in her arms. I wrap mine around her and hold her close, kissing the pile of curls on the crown of her head. "They were good days, for sure," I reply, recalling how, as teenagers, we'd have sex anytime and anywhere without a care in the world. But as amazing as that was, having Haven in a bed with blankets and real walls around us is much more preferred.

Haven rests her cheek against my chest. "You're different, you know."

I snort. "I hope so. I think I lasted about three minutes tops back then," I reply with a laugh, though it's not that far from the truth. Haven was gorgeous even back then, and I'd get so worked up the moment I touched her body that I'd only be able to last minutes.

"Well," she replies, batting her eyelashes, "your stamina has definitely improved, but so have your moves." She waggles her eyebrows suggestively and gives me a grin laced with naughty intentions.

I can't help it. I rub my hard cock against her stomach,

my brain short-circuiting at the glorious friction. "I have so many moves I want to show you," I whisper, running my open mouth down the slender column of her neck.

She gasps as she turns her head, seeking out my own neck. Haven runs her tongue over my Adam's apple and nips at my flesh. "Would these moves happen to be ones you can show me in the shower?"

"Fuck yes," I state, shoving the plate of pancakes in the microwave before tossing her over my shoulder and carrying her toward my bathroom. My hand lands hard on her bare ass. Her yelp is immediately followed by a moan of pleasure as my palm soothes the sting.

When I set her feet down, her hands instantly dive for the belt on my khaki pants. I rip the shirt she's wearing up and over her head, exposing her pert tits and her tight little body. Fuck, I'm already so hard I can't see straight. This morning might be a three-minute ride too.

The moment we're both naked and tumbling under the shower spray, I turn her around and press her into the tile wall. "Hang on tight, Have. This is going to be a fast, hard ride."

* * *

My mind has been reeling all week. I've been in a fog all morning, my thoughts continually returning to the woman who shared my bed.

"Come on, Daddy!" Chloe hollers from the doorway where she's been standing and waiting for the last few minutes. Now, when I walk around the corner, she's tapping her foot on the floor and giving me a pointed look. "You're being too slow!"

I laugh and scoop up my daughter as I walk by. With

the front door secured, we head to the truck and pile in. "You want to stop and get some groceries before we go?" I ask, fighting the smile that's threatening to spread across my face.

"No, Daddy! We need to go now and get the eggs!" she demands, anger marring her usually sweet little features as I stare back at her from the rearview mirror.

I finally laugh and start the truck, throwing the shifter into reverse and backing out. Chloe has been looking forward to today all week. After she got back from the zoo, she's talked about nothing but animals since. The zoo animals transformed into the barnyard animals at the Decker farm, so Haven talked to her parents, and they thought Saturday was the perfect day to bring Chloe for a visit. That's where we're headed.

I'm thrilled to see my daughter interact with the animals, but I'm probably more excited to see Haven. She had a few classes throughout the week, which kept her busy until dinner time. We had her over twice for a short visit, but she hasn't spent the night since Monday. And last night was an away football game, so I didn't get to see her in the stands. As much as I want her as an active part of my life, I still want to make sure we do things right, and I'm worried Chloe waking up and seeing Haven in my bed might be a step my daughter's not prepared for.

But I hope to talk to her about that today.

She's headed back to her mom's this afternoon, so now is the perfect time to feel her out.

"Hey, Chloe?" I ask, making my way through town.

"Are we there yet?" she asks, her face full of excitement.

"Not quite yet, sweetheart. Just a few more minutes." I adjust myself in my seat. "I have a question for you. About Miss Haven."

"She's going to be there too, right?"

"She is, yes." I swallow hard. Why is this so difficult to talk to my daughter? "Anyway, I wanted to, well, I just wanted to ask if you like Miss Haven. Do you? Like her, I mean?" Jesus, I'm sweating.

"I love her, Daddy. She's my bestest friend, besides Kimmy at preschool who lets me pick my Barbie first. And we share grapes because it's good to share, right, Daddy?"

"Yes, baby, it's good to share. And I'm really glad you like Miss Haven."

"Can we get pizza with her later?"

"No, not tonight. You're going to Mommy's after we see the animals, and you'll stay with her for two nights," I say, turning off the roadway and heading toward Haven's country home.

"Yay! But will you have pizza with Miss Haven tonight?" she asks innocently.

"Yeah, I will probably take her to a nice dinner somewhere."

"'Cause that's what boys do when they love girls?"

She's making this easier than I expected.

"Actually, yes, that's what they do. It's always good to spend time together. Is that okay? If I spend time with her?"

"Yep, Daddy! 'Cause you're gonna marry her, like Mommy and Dave. And then I can be the big sister, but only if I gets a little sister. I don't want a smelly brother."

I can't help but laugh as I pull into the Deckers' farm. I park out of the way by the barn, turn off the ignition, and hop out of the truck. The moment my daughter is unbuckled with both feet on the ground, I crouch down and meet her eye. "Are you okay with me going to dinner with Miss Haven? And having her at the house?"

"Can she sleep in my room, Daddy? We can snuggle in my bed," she asks with big, innocent eyes.

Grinning, I reply, "She'll have more room in my bed though. You like to kick, remember?"

"Oh, right!" she declares. We both turn toward the house and see Haven headed our way, a picnic basket in her hand and a wide smile across her stunning face. "Can I go now?"

I place a kiss on Chloe's forehead. "Yes, sweetheart, you can go now."

She takes off like she's shot from a gun and practically knocks Haven over when she reaches her legs. I trail slightly behind as they walk hand in hand toward the big barn, Haven telling Chloe all about the animals they have. When we reach the barn, Mr. and Mrs. Decker are there and pause from the chores they're doing to offer polite greetings.

Chloe listens intently as Haven takes her from the horses to the goats before finally heading back outside to the large coop behind the barn. "Are these the chickens?" my daughter asks, her eyes dancing with excitement.

"They are," Haven confirms, releasing the latch and opening the gate.

"Daddy, look! Chickens!" Chloe hollers, heading over to where they roam freely in a large fenced area. The moment she gets close to any, they flap their wings and run away.

"You've made her entire day," I say to Haven as I step up beside her.

She's grinning, her eyes watching my daughter try to catch a chicken. "She has made mine," she whispers.

"Daddy, do you see that one? He looks like my chicken at home."

"You're right, he does," I confirm, as Haven's mom, Barb, comes out of the main barn with a small bucket.

"Are you ready to help collect eggs? I saved some just for you, sweet girl," she says as she enters the fenced-in area. Barb takes Chloe over to the coop and shows her how to retrieve the eggs. She hangs on Barb's every word, doing exactly as she instructs.

"Would you like to get dinner tonight?" I ask, keeping one eye on my daughter.

Haven steps up beside me and leans her head against my shoulder. "I'd love to. Will Chloe be joining us?"

I shake my head. "She's with her mom until Monday. We get the rest of the weekend," I answer, wiggling my eyebrows suggestively.

The most breathtaking grin spreads across her face. "That sounds nice, but we could just stay in if you'd prefer."

My cock jumps in my pants. "As much as I'd love to keep you locked in my room all weekend, I'd rather take you to dinner first so I can show you off. How about the steakhouse on Main Street?"

"Oliver's? Do they still serve that hash brown croquette?"

"God, yes. My stomach just growled thinking about it," I confirm. "Do you remember ordering a bunch of those to-go, grabbing chocolate milkshakes, and heading out to that hill back behind your parents' barn?"

Haven's moans of pleasure remind me of the noises she made Monday night. "Those were the best nights. Until the mosquitos," she adds. Those damn pesky bugs always loved her sweet skin, almost as much as I did.

Do.

"Do you want me to pick you up or would you like to meet at my place?"

"How about I just come to your house. That way, my car is there in the morning." She blushes and looks around before adding, "Well, I'm assuming I'm still going to be there in the morning."

I pin her with a smoldering look. "Sweetheart, if I had my way, you'd never leave. Not my arms and certainly not my bed."

Haven leans against my shoulder and exhales. "I wish things would have been different for us, Bash. I wish I had stayed here. With you."

Everything around us just fades away when I turn and pull her into my arms. "Don't say that, Have. As badly as it hurt when you went to New York, that's who you were at the time and what you needed. You became a successful, brilliant dancer. You followed your dream, and you couldn't have done that here. Plus, there's Chloe. Our life together may have been different, but I wouldn't have her if you'd have stayed. So, don't regret your past, sweetheart. Appreciate it for what it taught you, but always keep your eyes forward on the future."

"On you?" she whispers, and my heart practically jumps out of my chest.

"Yeah, on me. And Chloe. And your parents, who are here. And the dance studio in town with the little ballerinas who look up to you with stars in their eyes. Just keep moving forward," I tell her, pulling her into my arms and kissing her forehead.

"Daddy, look! Eggs from the chickens!" Chloe bellows as she runs our way. One of the chickens runs in front of her and trips up her little legs. When she stumbles, she drops the egg in her hand, and it breaks. "No!" She instantly starts to cry for the broken egg.

Before I can move to the gate, Haven's already there,

releasing the latch and making her way to my daughter. Haven crouches down and takes Chloe into her arms and holds her tight. When she pulls back, she wipes the tears away and whispers, "It's okay, Chloe. Accidents happen, especially with eggs. I dropped one just the other day, and when I was younger, I'd drop at least one or two a week."

Chloe sniffles and wipes at stray tears. "But, then the chickens won't grow more chickens."

"These aren't going to the incubator, honey. These are eggs we eat for breakfast."

Chloe seems to be thinking awfully hard for a few seconds before adding, "Can I take some eggs for breakfast?"

Haven smiles. "Of course. Would you like to pick out twelve to put in your own carton?"

Chloe nods and grins, the sadness of dropping an egg long forgotten. "Can I take them to Mommy's?"

"Sure can. How about you pick out twelve for your mommy's house and twelve for your daddy's house?"

"Yes!"

"Come on, sweet girl," Barb says, reaching her hand for Chloe to take. "We'll go take all these eggs into the house and pick the ones you want to take home."

My daughter practically darts for the house—Barb and the big basket of eggs hot on her heels.

"Thank you for this. I'll pay for the two dozen eggs," I insist, but Haven just tsks.

"Like Mom will let you pay for any eggs."

"Well, I don't mind. I didn't bring her out here to take the product for free."

Haven waves me off dismissively. "Mom knows that." She glances around and reaches for my hand. "Wanna go for a short walk?"

I'm already grinning as I take her hand. "I'd go anywhere with you, Have. Anywhere."

* * *

"Right this way," the hostess says, smiling widely as she leads Haven and me to a table for two in the back. When she turns around, I can feel her eyes on me, but I ignore it.

"Thank you," my date coos, clearly noticing the hostess's appreciative glance my way, but just grins in reply. While I'm pulling out her chair, my hand brushes against her lower back, the contact making my blood start a southbound trip below my belt.

I nod to the hostess, who sets two menus down on the table before sauntering off to return to the front of the restaurant.

"God, this place hasn't changed a bit," Haven says as she deposits her napkin on her lap.

"Oliver's granddaughter took over but kept the menu exactly the same. She offers a few weekend specials, but all the staples her grandfather created are still here. Including the hash brown croquettes," I reply, glancing down at my menu.

"I'm having a steak," Haven declares without so much as glancing at her menu. She gives me a far-off grin as she asks rhetorically, "Do you know how long it's been since I've had steak?"

I close my own menu and set it on top of hers. "I'm guessing longer than you'd like?"

"God, I haven't had steak in years. Can you believe that?"

I reach over and grab her hand. "Well, you're having it now, right? It's part of the whole eyes forward on the future thing," I say, bringing her hand to my mouth to run my lips over her knuckles.

"I'm Dylan, your server. May I start you off with some drinks?"

"I'd like a white wine," Haven replies, while I order a beer.

"I'll be right back with those drinks and to get your order."

He returns a few minutes later with our drinks and takes our dinner orders. We both request the prime rib, prepared medium, with those delicious hash brown croquettes and steamed vegetables. Dylan takes off to place our orders and brings back our side salads and a basket of bread.

"I'm going to use the restroom. I'll be right back," she says, setting her phone down on the table and excusing herself to the opposite side of the restaurant.

After she leaves, I pull out my own phone and check for messages. There's one from a player about practice Monday, so I fire back a quick reply to his question. Just when I shove it back into my pocket, Haven's phone rings. It's some whimsical tune that reminds me of something she danced to during a recital in high school. I reach over for her device to silence it when I spy the word Home across the screen. Worried something's wrong with one of her parents, I slide my finger to accept the call.

"Hello?"

There's silence for a moment before the caller replies, "Is Haven available?" The tone is clipped with a northeastern accent.

"Uh, she's unavailable right now. Is there something I can help with?" I ask, trying to figure out who this could be, calling from home.

The caller sighs. "Tell her Leonard called. Her agent has been trying to reach her for the last week, but Haven hasn't returned her calls. It's about *Anything Goes*."

"*Anything Goes*?"

Leonard sighs. "The Tony Award-winning production?" he replies, as if I should have known right away what he was referring to.

"Okay," I start, rubbing my eyes.

"Listen, I know how Haven is. She's passionate and sort of jumps off the cliff without warning, which is probably why my girlfriend is with you and not at home in New York." Before I can reply to that, he continues, "I don't blame you for being attracted to her. Haven's gorgeous, but she's reckless and doesn't think. Much like this opportunity she'd let pass by just because she's shacking up with some guy in going-nowhere USA."

"Wow, tell me how you really feel," I mumble, trying to keep up with this pompous asshole's self-righteous spewing.

"This is the opportunity of a lifetime for her, and you're a fool if you don't see it as that."

"Aren't you the guy who cheated on her with her understudy when she was recovering from an injury?" I ask, unable to hide my irritation.

"New York is different than Podunk, Idaho. These things happen from time to time, but we don't let them derail us from the bigger picture."

"Which is?" I ask, leaning back in my chair.

"Haven belongs here, in New York. She's a dancer, plain and simple, and this is the opportunity of a lifetime."

"You mean, she belongs there, with you."

"That too. She'll be back, I know it. And if you knew what was good for her, you'd encourage her to call her agent back. *Anything Goes* will open more doors than you can possibly imagine, and let's face it, her career is limited. She's thirty-two, and everyone knows her body will start to change as she ages. These opportunities won't come knocking anymore and her career will be done."

I glance up and find Haven making her way toward me. "Well, Leonard, I promise to talk to Haven when she's available."

The pompous ass sighs. "Listen, I'm sure she's promising you all sorts of fairy-tale happily ever afters, but it's not real. She belongs here, performing on Broadway, with me and her friends. Not in Hope, Idaho, teaching little kids how to pirouette. *Anything Goes* would set her for life. Doors would open, but this chance has a deadline. Her chance. Don't blow it for her by keeping her there."

As Haven approaches the table, my heart climbs into my throat. "Thank you for calling. She'll be in touch." I hang up the phone and slide it back across the table to where I found it.

Haven looks confused. "Who was that?"

I clear my throat. "It said home on the screen, so I thought it was your parents. Apparently, home isn't the one in Idaho." My heart clenches and climbs up into my throat, making it hard to swallow. Hard to breathe. Hard to do anything other than ache. My whole body is tense as I take in the gorgeous woman across from me. The one I want but am not sure she's mine to have. At least not anything more than the temporary time we've already shared.

Her life is there.

Mine is here.

Realization crosses her face.

"Leonard called, Have. He wants you to come home."

CHAPTER 8

Haven

Taking a seat, I reach for my white wine and drain the glass before setting it on the table in front of me. "I've been ignoring his calls," I confess. I'm sure Sebastian thinks it's because I'm not ready to talk to him about what he did. That's not the reason. The reason is that I have nothing to say to him. Leonard is my past, and I intend for him to stay there.

Sebastian nods. "Care to tell me why?"

I shrug. "I don't have anything to say to him."

"Well, he certainly has things to say to you."

"I don't really care what he has to say, Sebastian." I watch him carefully, and I can see the indecision in his eyes. I left him once before, and although it's in our past, those wounds are still there. "I've been doing a lot of thinking about life and the future."

"Leonard seems to think that you're passing up the

opportunity of a lifetime." He watches me closely, gauging my reaction.

"That's his take on things."

"And what is your take, Haven? Is this job, this, *Anything Goes*, will it really shape your career?"

"My dance career in New York, yes, but not my career here in Hope." His eyebrows raise at my confession.

"All you've ever wanted was to be a dancer." His voice cracks, as his emotions shine through the armor he tries to wear. "I don't want you to give that up."

"You're right. I did want to be a dancer. I was young and thought that was the life, that living in New York and being on Broadway would be living the dream. I will be the first to admit I was wrong. So very wrong, Sebastian."

"Here you go." The server delivers our plates in front of us. "Can I get you anything else?" he asks as he places a bottle of steak sauce and extra napkins on the table.

"Can I have a glass of water, please?" I ask. I would love another glass of wine, but I need a clear head for this conversation. I need him to know that it's me making the decisions and not the alcohol.

"Me too," Sebastian says.

"Of course, I'll be right back with that."

"Eat, baby," Sebastian says quietly. "It's been years since you've had a steak. We can talk after."

That simple statement is why I will never leave this man again. He listens, and he takes what I want into account. I've only ever had that with Sebastian. Now that I've found it again, I don't want to let it go. Let him go. Not needing to be told twice, I dig into my steak. We're quiet while we eat, and I'm sure his mind is racing with how this is going to play out. What he doesn't realize is that our life was mapped out for us years ago; it's just finally being put into motion.

"Did you save any room for dessert?" our server asks. If he can feel the tension between us, it doesn't show.

"No, thank you," I say, dropping my napkin onto my plate.

"Just the check, please."

"Sure thing." He pulls the check from his apron, and Sebastian hands him his credit card.

Five minutes later, we're in his truck headed to his place. I know I should probably wait until we get there, but I can't seem to hold the words in any longer. "Sebastian—" I start, but he shakes his head.

"We're almost home. Can we just... do this there?" He reaches over the console and links his fingers with mine. That's how we ride the rest of the way to his place. Silence surrounds us as I process what I need to say. His thumb caresses mine, and that simple touch, the connection to him and the way it makes me feel alive, is all that I need to know that I'm making the right decision. Even if things don't work out for us, this is my home. This is where I'm meant to be.

"You want something to drink?" he asks as we settle onto his couch.

"No. I want to talk." There's no more time for stalling.

He nods, and his shoulders slump just a little. "I'm listening."

"You were right when you said I always wanted to be a dancer. Being a dancer was who I was, or at least who I thought I was at the time. Turns out time changes you, and what you once thought you wanted more than anything isn't so important anymore."

"I don't understand."

"My heart shattered the day I left for Juilliard. I convinced myself I would regret it if I didn't go, if I didn't follow my dreams."

"I know." He nods. "I agreed with you."

"So, I went. With each day, I missed you with every ounce of my soul. That pain never really went away, but as the days passed by, I got better at hiding it." I take a breath and prepare to say the words that I've kept deep inside for longer than I care to admit. "It's been a while since I've been happy. In fact, if I'm being honest with myself, the last time I was truly happy and carefree was when I was with you. It took me coming home to you. It took coming back to the small town of Hope to see that being a dancer is no longer my dream."

I watch as he swallows hard. "What is your dream, Have?"

"You. You and Chloe. I know she's not mine and that she has a mom, but that little girl, just like her daddy, has wound her tiny hands around my heart, and the thought of leaving either of you tears me up inside. I won't do it again, Bash, I won't give up those I love for a dream that doesn't make me happy. I wasn't happy in New York."

"Are you happy now?" I can hear the caution in his voice, almost as if he's afraid of the answer.

I nod. "Yes. I never thought teaching dance would be fulfilling, but to see the faces of my students when they nail a lift or a turn, it's good for my soul. It's more than that. It's good for me. For the first time in years, I'm living, really living. I can have steak and pizza and whatever else I want without the fear that I'm going to be ridiculed for gaining an ounce. Professional dance is cutthroat, and honestly, I just don't want to do it anymore. It's too much stress, I have no life, and I'd have to leave you, have to leave home again, and that's something I'm not willing to compromise on. You did taste that steak tonight, right?" I ask to lighten the mood a little.

He smiles and nods. "So, you're staying for your students?"

"And other things. I'm actually buying the studio. Mrs. Simone has decided it's time to retire. She called and asked if I was interested in buying her out, and I said yes."

"What?" He moves to the edge of his seat. "When did this happen?"

"A few days ago. It all happened pretty quickly, and I wanted to surprise you."

"Haven." He reaches his hand out for mine, and I take it, letting him pull me close to him. "Tell me I'm not imagining this. Tell me what this means," he says, placing a kiss on the back of my hand.

"I'm staying, Sebastian. Here in Hope. I'm not going back to New York. I don't know what that means for us, but I'm not leaving. I'm here, and if you want me, I'm yours." The words are barely out of my mouth before he's slamming his lips to mine.

"I want you. All of you. We didn't get our chance then, but now... now it's our time, Haven." The words are barely out before he's kissing me again, harder this time than before. His hands roam over my body, and I move in closer. I can never seem to be close enough to him. His lips trail down my neck, distracting me. That's why I'm squealing when he lifts me into his arms and carries me down the hall to his room.

"I want to take my time with you, but I can't. Not right

now. I was convinced you were leaving me, that you were going back to New York, and now you're telling me that you're here for good. That you're never leaving me again, and I need you, Haven. I need to feel your warmth wrapped around me."

"I'm yours." My hand rests against his cheek. "I'm home, Sebastian."

"Thank fuck." He sets me on the bed and takes a step back. "I need you naked. Now." I watch with rapt attention as his hands grip the hem of his shirt, and he pulls it over his head, tossing it on the floor behind him. "Haven." My name is a growl from deep in his throat.

"Sebastian," I taunt him.

Hand on the back of his head, he blows out a breath. "Baby, you just told me you were home, that you were mine, and I'm barely holding on here. I need you out of those clothes."

"Oh, these?" I sit up and pull my shirt over my head.

"Yes." He swallows hard.

Reaching behind my back, I unclasp my bra and let the straps slide over my shoulders before tossing it on the bed. "And these?" I ask, popping the button on my jeans and working the zipper. Lying back on the bed, I lift my hips and shimmy out of my jeans. They get stuck at my ankles, and Sebastian takes pity on me, grabbing them and pulling them off.

"Now who's wearing too many clothes?" I ask him.

Seconds. That's all it takes is a handful of seconds before his jeans and boxer briefs are lying on the floor. I give him my full attention as he grips his hard length and strokes himself. I lick my lips in anticipation, and another growl comes from him. "Haven." The heat in his eyes sends a rush through me.

Placing my index finger under the waistband of my panties, I tug and stop. "I guess I'm going to need some help." I'm lying. We both know that I'm capable, but the fire that burns in his eyes, I crave it like nothing ever before.

"My pleasure." Before I realize what's happening, he grips my panties and tears them from my body. "Finally," he whispers, as if he's been waiting a lifetime for me to be lying naked in front of him. I guess in a way he has. We both have. We've held onto the love we shared all those years ago, and here tonight, it's stronger than ever before.

Sebastian crawls up on the bed as I move back farther. It's as if he's the predator, and I'm the prey. Not that he needs to catch me. I'm all his. When his lips capture mine, I give him everything I've got. I open for him as his tongue duels with mine. There has never been a moment in my life where I've felt this kind of need to be closer to another person, to feel as though he's a part of me. Without warning, he pushes into me, and I couldn't stop the moan that falls from my lips if I tried.

"Welcome home, baby," he breathes against my lips as he begins to slowly pull out and push back in.

"I thought you said this would be fast?" I goad him.

"You want fast?" he asks, increasing the speed of his hips as he thrusts into me.

"Y-Yes," I pant, digging my nails into his back.

"Condom," he murmurs against my lips before he's pulling all the way out.

"No." He freezes. "I don't want anything between us."

"I'm clean."

"Me too. It's been months."

"Are you on the pill?"

I swallow hard before shaking my head. "No."

His eyes that were just moments ago blazing with

passion soften and fill with love. "You sure about this, Have?"

I nod. "Are you?"

"Yeah," he murmurs. "Maybe Chloe is going to get her little sister after all." He smiles down at me, and my heart feels as if it could burst with happiness and love.

This... this is what I've been missing. *He* is who I've been missing. He's all that I need. "Or a little brother," I say, placing my hand on his cheek. He leans into my touch.

"I say we give her both," he says, leaning over me, capturing my lips as he pushes his hips forward, and stills. "I love you, Haven. I've never stopped loving you."

There is no more talking as he shows me with his body, and with his lips, how much he loves me. We spend hours wrapped up in one another until we're both sated and exhaustion sets in.

* * *

"I can feel you staring," I say, burying my face in his neck. I've always been able to feel when someone was watching me.

"I've been waiting on you to wake up," he says, pressing a kiss to the top of my head.

"Someone kept me up until the wee hours of the morning."

His reply is a deep chuckle that rattles his chest as his arms tighten around me. "I have something for you."

"I need a break," I say, still exhausted.

I'm greeted with raucous laughter that echoes throughout the room. "No, not that, although when I'm anywhere near you, we're both ready," he says. I can hear the humor in his voice, and I can only imagine him wagging his eyebrows at me as he said it.

Pulling back from his chest, I look up at him. "What is it?"

"I came to see you."

"What? When?"

"In New York. It was after my first year of college. I found out that Juilliard was doing a showcase, and I hopped on a flight. I came to see your first show. I wanted to surprise you."

"Why didn't I know this?" I ask, sitting up, making sure to hold the cover over my bare chest.

"I sat in the audience, and I watched you, Have. You're an incredible dancer. Your talent blows my mind. I bought you flowers and waited for you."

"I didn't know."

He nods. "I saw you with a group of your dance friends, and you were smiling and happy. Your face was lit up, as it should have been. You just gave a stellar performance."

"Why didn't you say hello?"

"My palms were sweating, and I felt like I was going to be sick. It had been over a year since I'd laid eyes on you."

"I don't understand."

"You were happy. At least I thought you were happy. I didn't want to ruin that, so I stepped back. You and your group walked past me without you noticing."

"Oh my God." If it were possible to hear my heart breaking, it would be in this moment. I remember that night. I was smiling and laughing, but that was on the outside. On the inside, I was wishing that I could have shared that moment with him. "I wanted you there. I remember thinking that I wanted to share that moment with you."

"I was there, and you were incredible."

"A cruel twist of fate," I mumble.

"Why do you say that?" He tucks a strand of hair behind my ear. "Talk to me."

I can feel the hot tears prick my eyes, but I blink hard, keeping them at bay. "I would have walked away that night. If I had seen you, that would have been it for me. I was miserable, but I kept telling myself I was just homesick and needed a little more time to get over you. If I had seen you, I would have packed up and left with you."

"I was there to give you this." He opens his palm, and in the center lies a white gold ring, with a single sparkling solitaire diamond. "I had a scholarship, but I didn't need to work. However, I did. I saved every dime to buy this ring. I wanted you to follow your dream, but I wanted you to know I would be there with you every step of the way. I didn't know how we were going to make it work. All I knew was that I was broken without you. We'd talked about getting married and starting our lives, and well...." He nods toward the palm of his hand.

The tears I've been trying to keep at bay run freely down my cheeks. "I-I don't know what to say. I can't believe you kept this."

"Yeah, I flew home and went straight to my dad and handed him the ring box. He didn't ask questions. He just took the box from my hands. I'm sure the look on my face said everything he needed to know."

"Why do you have it now?" I ask, staring at the shining diamond in the palm of his hand.

"I stopped by there this week, and without a word, Dad handed me the box. Not a single syllable was spoken, but again, it wasn't needed. He knows how I feel about you, how I've always felt about you. After last night—" He stops, closing his eyes.

"Bash" I can barely speak. I'm so overcome with love for this man.

"After last night, I knew it was time. I know that I'm not taking you away from your dream... that you chose to be here with me. I could never have lived with myself if you gave it all up for me."

"I'm not happy there. I'm not giving it up for you, but you are a big part of my happiness. You and Chloe, my parents. I miss home."

I watch as he moves to climb out of bed and motions for me to come closer. Awkwardly, with the blanket held tight to my chest, I move to the edge of the bed. He hands me his T-shirt from last night before sliding into his jeans. With my hands clasped tight in his, he pulls me to stand and drops to his knees.

"Sebastian," I whisper as tears begin to rain down my face.

"I love you, Haven. I more than love you, but I don't know how to explain it to you. I don't have the words, but I'm going to try. I fell in love with you when I was a kid. I didn't know anything about living life, or being a parent, or making a relationship work. However, I did know that it was you. It's always been you. In my wildest dreams, I never could have imagined that we would be here in this moment, but we are, and I'm seizing the opportunity. I don't want another moment to pass by without you by my side. I want our forever, baby. Haven Decker, will you take my last name and help me raise my daughter? Will you have more babies with me? Will you grow old with me? Will you do me the incredible honor of being my wife? Will you marry me?"

I can't see him through the tears, but I nod, knowing he'll see me. I can't speak from the emotions clogging my throat.

"I need your words, Have," he says, his tone gruff.

"Y-Yes. Yes! I'll marry you," I say, finding my voice.

He stands, wrapping his arms around me tightly. I don't know how long we stand here holding onto one another, holding onto our future, but it's guaranteed to be a moment that neither one of us will ever forget.

EPILOGUE

Sebastian

Six months later

"Daddy, Daddy, let's go! We're gonna be late, and Miss Haven will be mad at us!" my daughter bellows from the open front door. I can practically see her tiny little foot tapping in frustration on the porch.

"I'm coming, sweetheart. Miss Haven won't be mad," I counter, locking the door behind me as I join her outside. The moment I do, she takes off for the vehicle and climbs in the back seat.

"Yes, she will. She's ner-bis for today and wants it perfect," she insists, buckling her seat belt.

"Nervous," I correct, securing myself in the front seat.

Haven is very nervous, though she has no reason to be. Today is going to be perfect. It's her first dance recital. I spent all morning at the gymnasium, helping her decorate and set up chairs. I left only long enough to pick up Chloe from Trina's house and stop by my house to grab the costume. Everything about today has been a cluster—from the time Trina got called into work and we had to completely rearrange our weekend schedule. Then I forgot the costume at my place, just adding another layer of chaos.

We drive to the gym, Chloe singing the song she's dancing to. I've heard it a thousand times in the last few months. The parking lot is already filling up, so I take a spot in the very back to leave better spots at the front for parents and grandparents. "Ready, Freddie?"

"I'm not Freddie. I'm Chloe!" My daughter giggles from the back seat.

Smiling, I grab the two fresh bouquets from the passenger seat and exit the truck. With my daughter's hand in mine, we head for the door that'll take us backstage. The entire room is full of laughing kids with happy giggles and excited eyes, and moms (and a few dads) trying to keep them under control.

"Let's get you changed," I say, glancing around for Haven but not seeing her yet. I'm sure she's fretting about some tiny detail or overseeing the VIP section in the very front of the gym.

We head over to the dressing area with curtained rooms for changing. This isn't something the previous owner had ever done, but after talking to Haven, she felt it necessary. Not every little dancer brings a mom backstage. Some have dads with them, and he can't exactly go into the little ladies' bathroom to help. So another mom is usually enlisted to assist a little girl get into a tricky costume since they're usually unable to do so themselves. I bought a PVC pipe and Haven made cheap curtains out of discounted table-cloths and old material. The end result is private dressing rooms where dads can help their daughters get ready for today's big day. We can tear them down and store them at the studio to reuse next year.

I help Chloe into her pink tights and black leotard. The tutu is her favorite part though. It's black with tons of sparkles that shimmer when the lights hit it. "Is Mommy going to make it?" she asks as I lace up her ballet slippers.

"Your mommy wouldn't miss this if she didn't absolutely have to, sweetheart." I stop tying and find her gaze. "You are the most important person in your mom's life. You know that, right?" Chloe nods. "But your mom is also a superhero at her work. If someone comes into the hospital who's really sick, Mommy may not be able to get away as quickly as she would like."

"Because she has to help the man who's sick."

"That's right. She plans to be here, okay, but if she can't, it's because someone needed her really bad."

My daughter seems to think about that for a few seconds. "I hope Mommy can help them if they're sick, because Mommy is the bestest nurse I know."

I smile down at her. "She is, you're right. And if she can't be here, you know Dave will be here, and he promised to video tape it for your mommy."

Chloe nods. "He said he'd cheer real loud for Mommy too."

My throat tightens.

Co-parenting isn't easy, and we don't pretend to have it all figured out, but it's times like these I thank my lucky stars that we're all on the same page. Dave is a good guy, and even though their schedules aren't easy to maintain, they make it work, still putting our daughter first.

"You bet he will be. I bet he cheers until his voice is

hoarse," I add, tickling her side when she's all set. "You ready?"

She nods. "Can I see Miss Haven? She has to put my hair up."

"Let's go out and see if we can find her. I'm sure she's getting anxious."

Chloe places her hand in mine and leads me out of the dressing room. I glance back, making sure we have all of our clothes in her bag, and worm our way through dozens of kids. I finally spot the woman I love over by the big velvet curtain, talking to the sound engineer. The moment she sees us headed her way, she smiles. It's one of relief and apprehension.

The first thing I do when I reach her is pull her into my arms and hug her tightly. I can practically feel the tension ebb from her body. "You have no idea how much I needed that," she whispers.

"I only left you for like a half hour. What happened?"

She just gives me a small smile. "The electronics for the curtain quit working. The school's maintenance man had to come work on it just as people started to arrive. The tablecloth for the desserts table arrived in blue instead of black, and the cake was late because the baker had a flat tire."

I hold her by the upper arms and just take her in. She's absolutely breathtaking in her own costume. It complements the ones the smaller kids are wearing. "Deep breath, Have. You got this." Then I place my lips against hers and savor the feel of her against my skin.

Chloe takes Haven's hand. "Do I look pretty, Miss Haven?"

The woman I love instantly drops to her knees in front of my daughter and smiles. "You are the most beautiful little ballerina I've ever seen." When Chloe grins from ear to ear, Haven adds, "Shall we pull your hair up in a pretty bun?"

Chloe nods big.

"Do you have your hairpiece?"

I dig it out of the bag and hold it while Haven works my daughter's hair up into a bun and adds the clip with the sparkly little top hat. It would have taken me twice as long to complete, and it probably wouldn't have looked half as good. I'm so relieved I didn't have to attempt that hairdo, and Haven clearly senses it.

"I got you, Daddy."

I kiss the side of her cheek and whisper, "Thank you."

She just beams back at me with those big eyes. "It takes a village...."

We only have a moment of calm before Chloe grabs Haven's skirt and gives it a slight tug. "Miss Haven?"

Again, she drops to her knees and gets eye level with Chloe. "Yes?"

"My mommy might not be able to come. She's at the hosbital."

Haven's smile is full of love and sadness. "I know, sweetie. If your mommy can't make it today, I promise we'll do something special for her, okay? I won't let her miss your big debut on stage, Chloe. Pinky promise," she whispers, extending her long pinky for my daughter to twist her much smaller one around.

Chloe grins a big, toothless smile and shakes her head. "Okay!"

"Now, are you ready to go out there?" Haven asks, standing up and dusting off her costume.

"Ready, Miss Haven!"

I glance through the now-open doorway and catch a big group of football players filing into the gymnasium. A smile instantly spreads across my face at the young men who have come to support my daughter during her big afternoon. She was there for them, cheering them on through the regular season and into post-season. We made it to the second round of playoffs before we lost to a tough South Mill team.

Adam is the last one to enter, but stops and turns before completely slipping out of sight. He gives me a big thumbs-up and a grin, and follows his teammates through the doorway. After the season, I was able to help Adam apply for some major financial assistance for the local community college. Now he'll be headed there this fall, preparing to take a few environmental science classes. He's working at the local hardware store now, and with the help of the Joneses who own the business, he's secured the studio apartment above the store.

Haven turns and claps her hands, drawing everyone's attention to the front of the room. She just gazes out on the dozens of faces, at her students, with pride and excitement. I reach for her hand and link our fingers together as she blinks back tears. Then she stands up tall and announces, "Showtime!"

* * *

Haven

The recital went off without a hitch. My little dancers were incredible, and my heart is bursting with pride for each of them. The smiles on their little faces solidify that I made the right decision. Never in my time in New York did I ever feel this amount of pride or accomplishment. All it took was coming home to see that.

Now that the recital is over, I can think about what I've been trying to push out of my mind all day. It was challenging to do, considering I spent the day with Sebastian. He was a huge help in pulling off the show, and I plan to thank him for it later tonight, right after I give him my news.

"Miss Haven!" Chloe runs as fast as her little legs will carry her, and I bend down to catch her when she leaps at me. "That was so much fun. Can we do it again?" she asks. Her little face is red from dancing, but her smile is bigger than I've ever seen it.

"We can, but it's going to take some time to learn some new dances," I tell her.

"Yay!" she cheers.

My phone vibrates in my pocket, and I pull it out to see a group message from Trina to both me and Sebastian.

Trina: I made it. I'm going to surprise her. Can you keep her occupied?

Me: You bet.

"I think Daddy has something for you," I tell Chloe, glancing up at Sebastian. He slides his phone back into his pocket, having just read the same message from Trina I'm sure.

"I do. Chloe, these are for you." He hands her a huge bouquet of flowers that are almost bigger than she is.

"Oh, Daddy, I love them. I wish Mommy could see them." Her face falls for the first time tonight, just as I spot Trina walking up behind her.

"Hey, Chloe, can you do me a favor?" I ask her. She bobs her head up and down, the sadness still lingering in her eyes. "Can you turn around for me?"

"You're silly, Miss Haven." She giggles but does as I ask. "Mommy! Dave! You made it. Did you see me dance? Did you?" she asks, jumping into Dave's arms. "Look, Daddy gots me flowers."

"I see that." Dave bops her on the nose with his index finger.

"Hey, glad you could make it." Sebastian holds his hand out for Dave.

"Wouldn't miss it."

"Mommy, did you take care of the sick people?" Chloe asks.

"I sure did, and I was still able to make your show. You need to teach me your moves," Trina says, making her daughter laugh.

"Am I at your house tonight?" she asks her mom. "I can show you when we get home."

Trina looks up at Sebastian, and he nods. "Yeah, sweetie, you can show me your moves when we get home."

"Daddy, I love my flowers." She holds them tight to her chest.

"And I love you. I'm going to help Haven lock up. You be a good girl for Mommy and Dave."

"I will. Love you, Daddy, love you, Haven."

My heart explodes with love for this little girl. "I love you too. You were great tonight, Chloe," I tell her. After a round of hugs, the three of them disappear into the now thinning crowd.

"Well, it's just the two of us. Whatever will we do with ourselves?" Sebastian asks, wrapping his arms around me and holding me close.

"I was hoping we could talk."

"Talk? Babe, you have to know that anytime a woman tells a man they need to talk, it's usually not a happy ending."

"Oh, were you hoping for a happy ending tonight, Bash," I sass back at him.

"Every night with you is a happy ending." He winks, and I throw my head back in laughter.

"Come on. I need to lock up. I arranged for us to come by tomorrow and pick everything up, and the cleaning crew I hired will be here first thing."

"Let's get you home then."

Home. His home, the one he shares with his daughter. I want nothing more than for it to be my home as well. Maybe once we talk, it will be. He insists that he follow me as we drive to his place. My nerves hit an all-time high for the day as I pull into the attached garage, in the space he claims is mine. Wiping my hands on my leggings, I grab my purse and climb out of the car. Sebastian is there waiting for me, sliding his arm around my waist and leading me inside.

"You hungry? Want something to drink?" he asks.

No way could I eat right now. "Not right now. Maybe a bottle of water, though?" I'm suddenly parched at the thought of the conversation we're about to have.

He grabs two bottles of water from the fridge, and laces his fingers through mine, pulling me into the living room. After placing the bottles on the table, he sits on the couch and pulls me onto his lap. I'm sitting sideways so that he can see my face. "Talk."

Here goes nothing. "I'm pregnant."

He stills. "Can you repeat that one more time?" he asks. His voice is gravelly.

"I'm pregnant." I let the words hang in the air between

us. His arms tighten around my waist, and I feel his stare, but I don't lift my gaze. Instead, I pretend that the pattern on his button-down shirt is the most exciting thing I've ever seen in my life.

"Have, baby, can you look at me?"

Knowing I can't hide from this, I lift my head, and what I see steals the breath from my lungs. He's smiling. Not just any smile. It lights up his face. "We're having a baby," he says reverently. His large hand slides over my still-flat belly. "This is what we wanted. All those years ago, we said we wanted kids."

"We have Chloe."

His eyes soften. "And now we're giving her a little brother or sister to love. I'm thrilled, and Chloe, she's going to be over the moon excited to be a big sister."

"She will," I say, tears welling in my eyes.

"How do you feel? Have you been to the doctor?"

"I'm feeling good. My breasts are a little tender, and no, I haven't been to the doctor. I was late, so I took a test."

"I want to be there. Every appointment, every milestone. We're in this together, Haven."

"I love you, Sebastian. I know it took us a little longer to get here, but there is nowhere else I'd rather be."

"I'm glad you came home," he says, pressing a soft kiss to my lips.

"I'll always come home to you," I assure him.

"You're damn right you will. After all, I'll be changing your last name."

THANK YOU

Thank you for taking the time to read, Home to You.

Be sure to sign-up for our newsletters to receive new release alerts.

Lacey Black
     http://bit.ly/2TVlfGK

Kaylee Ryan
     http://bit.ly/2tIVcrk

Contact Lacey

Facebook: http://bit.ly/2JBssXd
     Reader Group: http://bit.ly/2NWrRU7

Goodreads: http://bit.ly/2Y4Zzuw
BookBub: http://bit.ly/2JJhYnl
Website: http://www.laceyblackbooks.com/

Contact Kaylee

Facebook: http://bit.ly/2C5DgdF
Reader Group: http://bit.ly/2o0yWDx
Goodreads: http://bit.ly/2HodJvx
BookBub: http://bit.ly/2KulVvH
Website: http://www.kayleeryan.com/

MORE FROM LACEY

More from Lacey Black

Bound Together Series:
Submerged | Profited | Entwined

Rivers Edge Series:
Trust Me | Fight Me | Expect Me | Promise Me: Novella
Protect Me | Boss Me | Trust Us
With Me (Christmas Novella)

Summer Sisters Series:
My Kinda Kisses | My Kinda Night | My Kinda Song
My Kinda Mess | My Kinda Player | My Kinda Forever
My Kinda Wedding

Rockland Falls Series:
Love and Pancakes | Love and Lingerie
Love and Landscape | Love and Neckties

Burgers and Brew Crue Series:
Kickstart My Heart

Standalone Titles:
Music Notes | Ex's and Ho, Ho, Ho's
A Place To Call Home | Pants on Fire
Double Dog Dare You

The Driven World:
Grip

Co-written with Kaylee Ryan:
It's Not Over | Just Getting Started
Can't Fight It

Boy Trouble

MORE FROM KAYLEE

More from Kaylee Ryan

With You Series:
Anywhere with You | More with You | Everything with You

Soul Serenade Series:
Emphatic | Assured
Definite | Insistent

Southern Heart Series:
Southern Pleasure | Southern Desire
Southern Attraction | Southern Devotion

Unexpected Arrivals Series
Unexpected Reality |Unexpected Fight
Unexpected Fall | Unexpected Bond
Unexpected Odds

Riggins Brothers Series:

Play by Play | Layer by Layer
Piece by Piece | Kiss by Kiss

Standalone Titles:
Tempting Tatum | Unwrapping Tatum | Levitate
Just Say When | I Just Want You | Reminding Avery
Hey, Whiskey | When Sparks Collide
Pull You Through | Beyond the Bases
Remedy | The Difference
Trust the Push

Cocky Hero Club:
Lucky Bastard

Entangled Hearts Duet:
Agony | Bliss

Co-written with Lacey Black:
It's Not Over | Just Getting Started
Can't Fight It

Boy Trouble

ACKNOWLEDGEMENTS

ACKNOWLEDGEMENTS

To our Beta readers: Sandra Shipman, Joanne Thompson, Stacy Hahn, Lauren Fields, and Jamie Bourgeois. You ladies are the glue that helps hold us together. Thank you for taking the time from your lives, your families to read our words. Your time and input are invaluable to us. We will be forever grateful.

To our team: There are so many people to thank. We apologize if we've missed anyone. Here goes: Hot Tree Editing (Becky Johnson), Melissa Gill Designs, Kimberly Anne, Kara Hildebrand, Tempting Illustrations (Gel Yatz), Deaton Author Services (Julie Deaton)

Bloggers: Thank you for doing what you do. We know that you take time from your lives and your families to promote our work and we appreciate that more than you will ever know. Thank you for taking a part in the release of Just Getting Started.

Readers: Thank you for taking a chance on us. We are truly thankful to each of you.

To our reader groups: Lacey's Ladies and Kaylee's Kick Ass Crew. You are our tribe! Thank you for your never-ending support.

Manufactured by Amazon.ca
Bolton, ON